Two
Doctors,
Two
Loves

Also by Elizabeth Seifert

Two Doctors, Two Loves

ELIZABETH SEIFERT

DODD, MEAD & COMPANY

NEW YORK

Fic
Sei

2 3 4 5 6 7 8 9 10

Library of Congress Cataloging in Publication Data

Seifert, Elizabeth, 1897–
  Two doctors, two loves.

  I. Title.
PS3537.E352T9   813'.52   82-7436
ISBN 0-396-08101-0   AACR2

Two
Doctors,
Two
Loves

1

As a child, Helen had always thought of herself as an actress. A candidate for an Oscar, perhaps. She made up stories and played the female lead in all of them before an audience as imaginary as the story itself. She was not an only child. She was the middle one of four sisters, not so much neglected as ignored. Her older sisters were older by five and eight years. The youngest one, Amanda, was only fifteen months younger than Helen. Four girls, and Helen cutting out paper dolls, cutting off their heads and transposing them to change characters. She played in a corner of the basement of their home, played by herself. The older sisters were in school by the time she was born, the younger one was cute and lively and outgoing. A tomboy, their mother called Amanda. She was popular, she had many friends, and the family believed all the stories she told of the people she knew and the friends she had.

She did have some of them. Boys were crazy about Amanda. She would not go to college, but she was often seen on the campus grounds. Charlotte, the oldest sister, taught school and lived in Ohio for a time after she finished college. Adelaide did private tutoring and at times she

1

would be away from home, too, traveling with the families of her students. Students? Hardly. Spoiled, indulged children, attractive, but moved so much from place to place that a tutor in the home was the best solution. Helen thought of Adelaide as a servant in these big homes.

Helen liked school; she liked books, she played out the plots of stories. She loved her father who would take her with him when he drove his small car—a coupé it was called—if he needed to visit one of his plants at night. He was an engineer, supervising a dozen factories in or near the city. Helen could pretend that the coupé was a royal carriage, and her father, amused, went along with her fantasies.

Her father was a churchly man. He belonged to the cathedral chapter of their church. Helen went with him and became as familiar with the geography of the cathedral as she was with their neat seven-room home. She didn't talk much about the family to her father after she once asked why Charlotte had the biggest bedroom in the house. "Your mother wants Charlotte to have the best of everything," he had replied, speaking quietly. "Some mothers, I am afraid, have only one child. Your mother is a good woman."

But she had not wanted a big family.

Helen was a pretty child. Not so smashing-looking as was Amanda, who attracted everyone's attention, but a very pretty girl in her own right. Sometimes she thought her mother resented the prettiness of her two younger daughters. Amanda's vivacious good looks, her ability to wear almost any sort of clothes and look well. No. More than well. Smart was the word. Helen was particular about words.

She was the only blonde of the family. Her hair was a

pale gold, long, and with a slight wave. Her skin was perfect, her gray eyes watchful and thoughtful. Amanda could drive certain boys away by her stunning good looks; Helen did not frighten anyone. They all liked her, at school and down at the cathedral where she was popular with the choirboys, the children of the day care school, and the young postulants.

Their mother said that it was because Helen was jealous of Amanda that she married Jeremy O'Brien, whom she first met on the day of his ordination. He was a local boy; Adelaide had tutored him in Latin when he was fourteen, the only son of a wealthy family, long established in the city. He fell in love with Helen and married her. She supposed, thinking about it years later, that she fell in love with Jeremy. He was spoiled, he was not especially handsome—but an eighteen-year-old girl can be thrilled enough to marry a man six years older than she was, and go with him to live in the rectory of the church upstate, which he was building up to keep pace with the growth of the town and the church. Had she loved Jeremy? She was proud of him. She helped him where she could. She bore him a son whom he called Jared. She would have liked to name him for her father. But he was a darling baby with Helen's golden hair, and a dimple in his right cheek.

Her father, having wanted at least one son, was very proud of young Jared. "I am glad he has you for a mother," he told Helen, which puzzled her at the time, but which she later came to understand and treasure.

Helen regularly visited her family and Jeremy's. It surprised her, when Jared was two years old, for the young priest to say that they were going home for Christmas.

Helen had looked up at him inquiringly.

"I've resigned," Jeremy told her, and left the room.

3

Why? He had been doing well; he was popular in the church—but she asked no questions. She packed a few clothes for herself and a large suitcase for the baby, his playpen, his toys. Jeremy always made fun of the great quantity of gear it took to move a small child. But they went "home" for Christmas. There never had been a question of their going to Helen's home. When the baby was six months old, her father had died suddenly.

"But he saw him," Helen comforted herself.

So they were in the O'Brien home for Christmas dinner, having gone through the ritual of Christmas Eve service at the cathedral, Christmas morning breakfast, the opening of stacks of gifts. And the baby was tucked snugly into bed before the family and guests sat down to the beautiful table, the gleaming turkey, and the plum pudding, when Jeremy unexpectedly rose from his chair and announced that he was sorry to tell the family, cousins and aunts, nieces and nephews, that he was getting a divorce from Helen.

His mother had stood straight up. "Why?" she asked.

"I have my reasons. I—" He went on talking. Helen, shrunken back into her chair, was again playing with paper dolls, pasting one head on a figure, not caring for the effect and replacing it. . . .

People were watching her, listening to Jeremy. She never could remember just what it was he'd said. She lifted her head, brushed back her hair.

"You will stay here with us," said Jeremy's mother firmly. "My son may be dishonest. I am not. You and your son belong in this House." They always called it that, capitalizing the name.

And so things happened. She did belong in the House. She remembered the swirling pattern of the damask cloth on the dinner table that night; she remembered playing with Jared in the snow; she took him to the preschool of the church near the House. People were kind to her. When her mother died and left her estate to Charlotte and Adelaide, Helen asked only for a small bank into which her father had used to put the change from his pocket and later give to what he called the Little Sisters of the Poor.

The fog lifted and Helen made a life for herself. She made friends. Someone told her that Jeremy had returned to the priesthood; he had a church in the East. . . .

Jeremy's mother was good to her. Really good. And no one thought it strange that the House should become Helen's—*femme sole,* with a large sum of money to maintain it. She had certain milestones in her life which kept her busy, especially the growth of her son, a fine, quiet boy who studied medicine. She sewed and gardened, and worked for the church, and began to ask herself if she had ever loved Jeremy. Other men—no. She was too busy. And the bruise inflicted by one man never healed. He was killed in a sailing accident. The papers were filled with the accounts because by then Jeremy O'Brien was a bishop and some mention was made of his early marriage and divorce. Helen glanced at the headlines, folded the newspapers for the Scouts' paper drive. She was still a young woman, and still pretty. Amanda mentioned it to her in a letter, and a young worker in the Altar Guild asked her straight out, "Were you his first wife, Helen?"

"Yes," said Helen quietly, "I was."

"What happened?" asked the girl.

"Nothing," said Helen, smoothing the fair linen.

So much for the family. There was also a house. A personality in itself. The House. A member of the family, of the community.

It was a large house, a country home. Bought from a rich man who had built it to entertain the many relatives who came to America to see and celebrate one of the world fairs. That celebration over, Jeremy's grandfather had bought the House at a great bargain.

"Expensive to maintain," had said the builder, "and you can take the cupids and stuff from the ceilings."

"It's good farmland," had said Jeremy's grandfather. He was not about to say that he wanted the cupids and the roses. Of course, it was good farmland, on the river, and Jared, as a child, had loved the cherubs that adorned the ceilings. He gave them names and played with them. He still enjoyed them. Though he remembered deciding, as a young medical student, that no child like them would ever stand erect or walk. But—he liked them. And refused to consider their being painted over. When he was twenty-one, Helen had deeded the house to him.

It was a tall house, built on a high rise of ground, facing south, and it afforded a peaceful view of the gently rolling countryside, and the river.

The farmland had dwindled to ten acres or less of smooth lawns, trees, and flowering shrubs. Flowerbeds, which Helen developed and cared for. Verandahs, upstairs and down, stretched the full length of the housefront. There was a large chimney of unusual design, free standing from the house itself. The rooms were large and high-ceilinged, and the furnishings luxurious. The entrance hall opened into the dining room and was bound by an open staircase with a cubbyhole closet under the stairs, always Jared's most private place.

Flowers abounded always in the House.

Because it had been built for visiting Europeans, there

6

was a formal parlor, light and elegant in German rococo style with a strong French flavor supplied by the local craftsmen. The afternoon sun streamed through a large bay window and picked up the white and gold in wall details and Louis XV furniture.

Jared and his mother had continued to live there after the death of the grandparents, a quiet family, well known, but not seen too often in the city's big affairs. Helen was always a part of the social life, and Jared, as he became older, might have shared it. He attended a good college and declared for medical school, the youngest in the class. The year he was to enter he asked his mother if he could have the attic.

She looked at him in surprise. "You've always played up there," she said uncertainly. "What do you want. . . ?"

"I don't want to live near the hospital," he told her. "But I would like my own apartment. I'll clean it out this summer, and find ways to furnish it."

"We were going to England . . ."

"I've been to England. I would like the rooms, Mother."

She plucked a petal from the bowl of flowers on the table beside her chair. "I find it hard to refuse you," she said. "Is there a girl in the picture?"

This surprised him. "I don't know any girls."

"They know you."

He grinned. "How about the attic?"

"Of course. I could stay home and help you."

"I would rather try it alone. If I get into a mess, you'll know it when you come home and can straighten things out. This might cost a little money."

They had a joint bank account. Money had never been a problem. "Zenobia—" she said thoughtfully.

7

Zenobia was the housekeeper.

"Ivory says he'll keep me cleaned up." Ivory was Zenobia's son.

"All right then. Do we discuss plans?"

"I don't have any. Except to clear out the attic."

"Have a rummage sale?"

"I could." He was thoughtful. Both were thinking of the space under the wide hip roof of the tall house.

"Air conditioning," said Helen.

"Or I'd fry. Yes, air conditioning, and insulation for the roof. Two rooms, I think."

"And a bath."

So it was settled. When Helen returned from her six weeks' trip to England, largely on church business but made pleasant by friends, Jared had his quarters well in hand. Two rooms. A pleasant bedroom with, of all things, a half-poster bed.

"I don't know what I expected," said Helen breathlessly.

Her son laughed. "I didn't either," he admitted. The bed filled most of the pleasant room. There was a wide window seat—lamps—the House was not one to be filled with knickknacks and bric a brac. Surprisingly, a glowing Persian rug added color to the creamy, comfortable room. "Cozy," murmured Helen, touching the cane-seated rocking chair.

"Come see the other rooms," said Jared.

"A laboratory?"

"It may become one."

They went across a narrow hall, with a no-nonsense bathroom to one side. Helen touched and nodded to the old German silver sconces beside an older, and misty, mirror. "Did Adelaide . . . ?" she asked.

8

"Yes, she gave them to me," said Jared. "She said they were old."

They were. The mirror had hung in Helen's room in her father's house. She pressed her son's arm. "You're a comfort to me, Jared," she said softly.

"Wait till you see my sitting room."

"You have gone old-fashioned," Helen said laughing. Then she sighed. "It is a sitting room," she agreed. "And it is lovely," she murmured.

Dull yellow walls, a brassy green rug, and the warm woods of the Victorian furniture. There was another rocker, deep and inviting, couches against two walls, a table and three chairs between two of the windows. Flowered side curtains, sheer glass ones.

"I'm moving up here," she told Jared.

"Any time, lady. Any time."

That was the House.

The hospital. A huge institution of many units. Buildings of eight stories could seem small against the monstrous surgical center. Going from one department to another, doctors and nurses who had worked in the place for twenty years could get lost.

The people. Just as big, really. And one could get lost trying to guess the truth about the individuals. Doctors too often have two lives. A thousand doctors? Could one select a single one? Or two?

Take for instance, Dr. Jared O'Brien, microneurologist. Standing, late at night, working meticulously over the table on which lay a woman whose leg had been severed in an automobile accident.

This had occurred at three in the afternoon. It was now

9

midnight. Later. There had been the recovery of the patient, still conscious, her leg badly crushed.

The session in the emergency room where the new trauma center was ready for just such events. The patient was quieted, there was discussion, and Dr. O'Brien was sent for. People glanced swiftly at the bright-haired man who was the trauma center's new surgeon, and whose name was also O'Brien, Joel O'Brien. Someone ventured to ask if he knew the neurologist.

"I've not met him yet," said that Dr. O'Brien. He was watching his patient closely. The terrible shock and fighting had been quieted. But to attach a leg—

"Can he do this sort of thing?" he murmured to one of the other doctors.

"Jared? He often does."

Jared came; the first Dr. O'Brien watched him closely. "I've heard of him," he murmured to himself. "I've heard . . ."

The famous neurologist studied charts, he examined X-rays, he talked to the patient, who was semiconscious. She held her gaze to his face, one side of which was covered from eye to chin with a silvery mask or patch.

Could this be the great one? The miracle worker she had heard talked about? "You're not very old," she whispered.

"You aren't either," said the doctor pleasantly. "May I try to attach your leg?"

The patient nodded and drifted off into unconsciousness.

At four o'clock the next morning, he dropped his gown and mask in the can, and stood for a minute realizing how tired he was. Every line of his body slumped. So much had been done. He had supervised the preparation of surfaces. Blood had been tested and a supply readied. Preliminary "fancy work," as Jared called it, was performed. The doctor had even slept for an hour. But most of the time, he worked, standing tall, his fingers as delicate as those of a skillful woman; his instruments were tiny, his assisting team skilled. They—and Jared—used jeweler's tools, watching their behavior through glasses that were really pairs of powerful microscopes as, inch by inch, they reattached muscle tissue, blood vessels, and nerves.

The new trauma surgeon came up and watched for a time. "Does he do much of this?" he asked in awe.

"Hundreds. From a fingertip to a whole foot."

"I heard he rejuvenated vasectomies."

"That, too. It's a delicate maneuver."

"He's good."

"He is *very* good," said his companion.

"Why the face patch?"

"What face patch?"

The younger man shrugged. "I can tell he's one of the adored ones."

"Look, Doctor . . ."

The trauma O'Brien lifted his hand. "I came here to join the crowd," he said. "And from what I've seen, it won't take trying."

The surgeon elected to sleep at the hospital; without going to sleep, he would never make the twenty-mile drive home. But he was up again at eleven, "just to see if you guys were doing things right."

They evidently were. His patient, heavily sedated, was in good shape. "That quick trauma attention helped," murmured Jared, as he wrote on the charts.

"His name—the new chap in trauma surgery is named O'Brien, too."

Jared nodded. "It's a common name. Fairly common. I'll bet we have half a dozen O'Briens here on the roster."

"He spells his as you do."

"Mhmmmnnn. I'm going to shower, make rounds, and go home. See that you don't let anything go wrong here."

"We'll try, Doctor."

But they did go "wrong." Before Jared had finished rounds, word of a kidney transplant came in for a baby they had been keeping alive for two weeks waiting for a donor. So Jared went back to work, shaking his head when someone asked if his fingers didn't get tired.

"My back does," he said. "My feet."

The whole O.R. staff agreed on that. Their feet got tired, too.

Severed limbs; vasectomies for men who had changed their minds and wanted the scar opened; function restored by kidney transplants—he wished he could get more of them; and a student from the university exploring the cliffs above the river fell and everybody, the young man told himself aloud, had a hell of a time with that one. To get down the steep, rocky slope to him, to quiet him, to get his limbs examined—"counted 'em all," murmured Jared, who was "great on talking to himself." If anyone answered or commented, it seemed to startle him. "Fine man down in emergency," he murmured now. He intended to stop in there and tell the other O'Brien so. But it was six o'clock before he made rounds, wrote orders, and had been told three times to go home and go to bed.

"May I leave my bleeper here?"

"Oh, Doctor . . . "

"Just tell the page clerk it's out of order." He strode toward the elevator and the garage, and the car, and the road home.

Then he sighed.

His mother was waiting on the verandah, the sun slant-

12

ing across the river, the lawn, and seeming to settle in her silver-gold hair. Jared bent to kiss her.

"Long day?" she asked, holding his hand warmly.

"And night, and another day. Can we eat out here? I washed my hands before I left the hospital."

"I'll tell Zenobia. She's been promising that you'd wear yourself out."

"And good old Zenobia never misses." He watched his mother go into the house. A tall and slender woman, her hair beautiful, her face serene. He looked at the river. It too was quiet and enduring. The flowers in the garden were fragrant.

"He'll be half asleep," Helen told Zenobia when they were ready to bring the trays out to the verandah.

"And we'll jest let him sleep," decided the large, generous woman who had cared for Jared since he was a baby, come to spend Christmas with his grampa.

But Jared was sitting on his heels beside Helen's needlepoint bag, threading needles. He did that regularly for his mother. "It's the only practice I get," he would say, explaining his dexterity. "You need to get more yellow yarn. What are we making?"

"Cushions for the communion rail," said Helen. "Come now, and eat Zenobia's good dinner."

Jared cast a swift smile at the big woman in white. "I had chipped beef for lunch," he warned

She sniffed. "Ain' never cooked you chip beef in my life," she asserted.

"I'll bet you'd make it taste good," he assured her. "But I'll manage tonight with lamb chops."

"You'd better," his mother advised. "Have you any idea what lamb chops cost?"

13

"You got your name in the paper this mornin'," Zenobia told him.

Helen looked up, surprised. "How did that happen?" she asked. "You told me you were working, Jared."

"That way he got his name in the paper, Miss Helen. Wait." Zenobia fished in the pocket of her uniform. "Ivory found it."

"He always reads the funny papers," Jared murmured.

Helen laughed. Her laughter, her beauty, her whole appearance were younger than the sum of what her years must be. "What did the rascal do, Zenobia?" she asked as the housekeeper handed her the clipping.

Helen read the paragraph or two. "My favorite microsurgeon," she said to Jared.

"You're partial."

"I am. Will it succeed, Jared?"

"Too soon to tell. Don't talk shop, Mrs. O'Brien."

"No, Doctor. I won't."

"Another O'Brien in the hospital?" asked Helen. "Offering competition?"

"I doubt it. Though I'd call it help and would welcome it. This man is in a new field. Rape and other trauma emergency surgery."

"Yes."

"Some badly injured people come into emergency and fight like hell. It takes a big team, extreme measures. Blood transfusions. It is very important to get such a patient quieted and ready for care. An ambulance with such a patient will pass a regular hospital to get to one with the service. Here comes dessert and I'll bet a dime it's dishwater pudding."

Helen laughed. As a very small child Jared had so called the lemon sauce that Zenobia made and poured over plain

14

cake. At first both his mother and grandmother had protested the name. But it fit the appearance of the sauce and
Jared was nothing if not persistent.

Now Zenobia looked at him fondly, "You wearin' a hospital shirt," she said accusingly.

"I ran out of good ones. Besides, it's clean."

"'Tain't ironed."

"Come up to date, Zenobia. New materials don't need
ironing."

"They need it but they don't get it."

"All right. All right. Fix me a stack of ironed shirts to take
back. The used ones are in my car."

"You do know how to handle women," said Helen. "I
can't imagine why you haven't married one."

"Why should I? With you and Zenobia to take care of
me?"

"We'll leave it at that," said Helen.

But she knew why. It was that dreadful scar with which
he had survived the war in Vietnam. She herself had never
seen that scar. When her son kissed her, he always pressed
his left cheek against hers. She sighed. He seemed happy.
He enjoyed his beautiful home. He seemed satisfied with
his attic quarters where he had music at the flip of a switch,
a library at hand. But because of that scar, Jared had almost
no social life, and no women friends.

"Look up your trauma man," she said when they rose
from the table. "Another O'Brien might be interesting."

"I'll do it. We need a good trauma man."

Helen sighed. She had been thinking of a friend, not just
another doctor.

The nurses at the hospital also wished for other things to
enter Dr. O'Brien's life.

Watching him at work, alert to help when needed, they

thought, or sometimes murmured to one another, "He's handsome. Even with that patch, even in greens, he's handsome."

"And a dedicated doctor in every way," the companion might say. "The other night, doing that leg replacement, staying all night on the job didn't bother him. He was where he'd rather be than anywhere else."

Both young women sighed, remembering that long night, the doctors, the assistants, the pathologists and blood specialists, the crowded operating room which got a little hot. Everyone busy, everyone closely conscious of the tall doctor who was the center of the scene. Alert to any change in the sounds that surrounded him. The least bleep, the hurrying of a process, the sigh of a young intern unaccustomed to these all-night jobs.

"He was where he would rather be than anywhere in the world," said the first nurse.

Remembering that long, long night, Jared might have told her that he'd been wishing he was at home, back under the silky, warm blanket that Helen had brought him from Peru, where she had gone on a cruise last spring; he'd have a good book propped against his knees, a tart apple to bite into . . .

Only—the nurse was right. He *was* exactly where he wanted to be, where he had trained and trained to be. This night, thinking back on the leg case, which was doing pretty well, and the kidney one, which was not, he thought the times through, even to the two nurses who talked about him. He knew that people speculated. Of course they did. He speculated about himself. He had carefully selected his field. Doing general surgery, a surgeon would comment on his dexterity, his ability to use small instruments, get into small places.

16

When vasectomies had become popular, he had been assigned to do them, thinking, then saying to his patients, "You'll be back."

The men did not believe him, but he had been right. Within five years they were back. He did a dozen, two dozen, fifty corrections. It was a delicate task of reconstruction. He had the instruments, he had the delicate skill. He became famous. He was called the world's leading microsurgeon. He knew there were others. Just as good. Some not good at all. And often he was asked to make a second try. "I'm no magician," he always warned. "The first chap must have tried all my tricks." But sometimes he could correct the damage done.

"It's the instruments," he said whenever he spoke at all of his work. "You have to have them small, and sharp, and right."

"And the hands and eyes . . . ," if it were a doctor to whom he was talking.

"That helps," agreed Jared. "I don't take the credit for that."

"Your most successful . . . "

Jared knew what he would say. He was the only doctor known to have transferred the testicle of one man to his twin brother. Then to have done it again . . .

"Wait and see if it works," he would tell those who offered him praise, honors . . .

It did work. One of the men's wives was pregnant. She promised to name the baby Jared.

He shook his head. "Don't do it," he said. "I've had my troubles."

But he was famous. His operating room always held an observing audience. He sometimes saw the other Dr. O'Brien there. "I must look that guy up," he told himself.

17

And, finally, he did go over to emergency. On the panel, he identified the doctors on duty. Yes. There it was. Joel O'Brien, M.D. Surgeon.

"He's a good-looking fellow," he told his mother that afternoon. "Dark blond hair, taller than I am, I think. A friendly way . . . "

"You liked him."

"I was curious because of the name. He seems to know his job. Emergency is no picnic."

"Like microsurgery," said Helen.

Jared glanced at her. "Like doing fine needlework for the church," he retorted. "Your job, my job, this fellow's job. He'd been to Nam, too, though he's quite a few years younger than I am."

"A child—"

"Mother!"

"I like to tease you, Jared. You get so solemn about things."

"Does he claim relationship?" asked Brig, who had dropped in during dinner, and eaten dessert. Brig, Brigadier General Morse, was a member of the church; he had worked on many projects with Helen. Retired from the Marine Corps, he liked to travel. Asking Helen to marry him had come early in their friendship.

"Jared needs me" she had told him.

"And you need Jared."

"Yes. Yes, I do. But you travel so much. Maybe—I do like you, Brig! Maybe we could figure a compromise, half travel, half here at home."

"With Jared always coming first."

"Yes. Yes, he always will."

So they were friends. The sisters did not approve. Some

18

of the church people, through jealousy perhaps, thought they saw too much of each other.

"You can't possibly please everyone," Brig advised her. "So try pleasing yourself."

It was good to have such a friend, and Helen thought they controlled the situation very well.

"Now!" she continued their discussion. "Tell us about this traumatic surgeon of yours."

"Traumatic!" Jared picked up a magazine. Helen rose and came across to take it from his hands. She sat down on the great green footstool beside the couch.

"He was a conscientious objector," said Jared, as if there had been no interruption. He and Helen were very good friends. "And he worked with this medical team. Not easy work, lady. When he came home he says he was dead tired, without enthusiasm for anything that he could do. He already had his M.D. and it was time for him to specialize, but he didn't know of a field that seemed interesting. He had handled everything in Nam—all came out alike, he says. I think he must have had a hard time getting established. But emergency rooms always need doctors, and he came here. We were expanding the trauma department and, to quote him, God knew he was familiar with that."

"I should think so. He sounds lonely. Why don't you ask him out here for dinner, or a weekend."

"Oh—"

"I know. He must rank pretty low in the staff pecking order. And he sounds as if he needed a root or two."

Jared looked at her and shook his head. "How you can get to the bottom of things!" he marveled.

"Also, it would be nice to have a second son."

Jared leaned back into one corner of the couch. "I never suggested— This fellow is no relation. O'Brien is a common name."

"It is. That's why you have a common name. He is your half-brother."

"Mother . . . "

"I've done a little looking up myself. Through the Auxiliary, my volunteer work. And he's not more handsome than you are. Hasn't he told you that he is your brother?"

"No. Nor have you told me about your snooping. Anyway, I don't believe you."

"Because he didn't mention it? Put yourself in his place, Jared. If you were down and out—to a degree—would you make claims on your more fortunate— Would you tell—?"

"And my mother wouldn't tell me, either. Only now she will."

"Don't you want me to?"

Jared shrugged, and turned to lift his legs so that he could rest stretched on the couch, his head on the cushions piled against one arm. Helen would have loved to stroke his hair, but she had learned not to touch his head.

"Are you going to tell me?" Jared prompted her.

For a time she said nothing. The perfume of the chestnut tree in flower came through the open bay window. The big room glowed softly in the light of late evening. Jared closed his eyes. "I might as well sleep," he said.

"Yes, do," his mother retorted. "Charlotte has told me often that the day would come . . . "

"Let Aunt Charlotte be," said her son. "The aunties resent your marriage and your fine big son."

Helen laughed softly. Her sisters did resent those things. "I had married," she said softly, "and your father wanted a divorce. I was shocked, and so were they."

20

"I've heard."

Helen was not about to speak again.

Jared's eyes rolled upward to her face. "Why?" he said. "Why did he want a divorce? He was a priest of the church."

"He was. And a very good one. But—he divorced me, and was not given another church for five years. I was very young—and you were two."

"And the cutest little nubbin," said Jared in a droning voice.

"You were!" his mother insisted. "Why he didn't want us is an entirely different story from the point of view that we are using this evening. Your grandparents insisted that I stay here with you. It seemed a pleasant alternative to even a brief return to my sisters in their home."

Jared made a sound half profane, half pained.

"Your grandfather was a very rich man, he had this big house. You were adored by him and your grandmother. And they persuaded me that having us here somehow dulled the shame of what their son had done."

"Was there another woman?"

"There was, but we won't speak of that."

They never had spoken of it.

"But he did marry again," said Helen. "Later a kind and lenient bishop gave him the right to preach again and serve the church. I read in *The Living Church* that he had a son. This must be that son."

"A doctor named Joel O'Brien," murmured Jared.

"You know that your father became a bishop of the church."

"I know. I never saw him."

"Your fault, or his?"

"Mutual consent, I suspect. Anyway, I was busy. Medical school, Vietnam for my residencies. I went into the marines, and meant to make a career of military medicine."

"And got half of your face blown off."

Jared's hand covered the patch on his cheek.

"I knew about your father's second son," said Helen. "That he was a conscientious objector, and I wondered if that did not shame or hurt your father."

"Did it make any difference at all?"

"Perhaps not. But this second son let himself be drafted; he was in medical school."

"He calls himself a failure there," said Jared. "He said that his father—our father—died during that time. I remember reading that my father had died. And I was ashamed that I cared so little. Did you know him, ever? The son, I mean."

"I never saw him. I would have told you."

"We have seldom spoken of my father. And perhaps now you should not acknowledge this brother so suddenly discussed."

There was a pause.

"I liked the fellow," he said softly. "I am in a spot to do things for him. Help him establish the traumatic emergency thing. . . . We might even become friends."

"You well might. You need friends, and perhaps he does."

"He's more outgoing than I am."

Helen rose from the stool. "Well, the choice has to be yours. It's your hospital, and this is your home."

Jared sat up and looked at his mother. "I'll bring him out here for dinner some evening. And you can tell him that I owe him half of my inheritance of this estate."

Helen's face flushed, then turned pale.

"There is no need. Dear, there—"

"He's a grandson, the same as I was."

"Your grandfather knew that he existed."

Jared looked astounded. "And so did you. Did you help him come to the hospital?"

"I knew that there was a stepson somewhere. That is all. If you like him, be kind to him, be friends. Do what you wish. But the will was specific. You were to inherit, and no other claims were to be made upon you or the estate."

She turned and walked from the room. Protecting her son? But this Joel was his brother—and if he seemed to like Jared and his mother—could they be friends? He would try a weekend, perhaps. Jared too needed friends.

Helen knew, because their family attorney was an old friend, that Jared had spoken of transferring some of his estate to Joel. Jared himself did not mention this move. He seemed to be very busy at the hospital, and there had been no dinner invitation issued, she thought. She did not mention that matter to him again. He would do as he promised when the right time came. The right time for him.

He had patients scheduled tightly from one week's end to the other. Ninety percent of his patients came from outside the vicinity. The operation that he did most regularly and that he had performed more than any other doctor was a microscopic vasectomy reversal, by which he altered previous sterilization surgery by sewing the severed tubes together again. He knew less than a ten percent failure in doing this delicate task. His waiting list of patients was almost a year long. The operation took two or three hours. To avoid failure, he had devised a procedure, practiced by no other microsurgeon, of cutting away any damaged tubes, adding thus to the length of time he must put to the surgery, and he had received worldwide attention for making the vasectomy reversal successful, though difficult even for so skilled a microsurgeon. The few stitches required to

23

rejoin the tube were made inside and outside of a vessel as small as a piece of thread.

Dr. Klopman, his assistant surgeon, said this tube was less than one third of a pinpoint. Actually, it was 1/300th of an inch.

Dr. O'Brien had his own operating room, his own team, and could say for himself how and when he would accept a patient, how and when he would operate. . . . Always he was ready to do a task like the woman's leg he had repaired, the kidney he had transplanted that same session.

The American College of Surgeons had asked to have a film made of his microsurgery, and this was shown to every prospective patient.

"It doesn't show your face," one man pointed out.

"Only hands are important," said Jared.

"I'd think they would be long-fingered and delicate. Yours look like almost any man's hands."

"They are like them. I've just learned to use them in conjunction with special instruments."

"And the glasses."

"Oh, yes. Those horror-movie spectacles!"

Joel saw the film. "How did you get him to make it?" he asked. "He's so—well, not shy, but he is reserved. He doesn't talk about his work."

"He'll answer any question," said Tucker, Dr. Jared's secretary, "if the person is—well—involved."

Joel was talking to himself. "He seems so human otherwise," he told the tall, handsome black man.

"Don't doubt that he is," said Tucker. "He's just a genius who found out what he could do best."

24

2

Helen did not again mention the matter of Joel's coming to the House. She went about her own affairs; she was a busy woman, with a big home to run, a busy doctor to whom she wanted to adjust her time. She did volunteer work in his hospital, she did church work—and she could always find time to sit with him on the verandah after a busy day.

But on her own she made herself known to Joel. He stood back and looked at her. "You can't be Jared's mother," he said.

"Oh, I have proofs." She was very pretty, with her pale hair and fine skin, her lovely eyes.

"I wish you could be friends with Jared," she said.

"I can be. He's so damn busy. Excuse me. I'm sorry."

She laughed. "He is damned busy. And it's only my sisters who would be shocked to hear such a mild cuss word. Your father used them."

Joel's face darkened. "Yes. He did," he said shortly. Then he excused himself and went down the hall. Helen watched him. She liked the young man. She wished. . . . Should she talk to Jared again? She would find ways to

25

speak to Joel. She could herself invite him out to the house, but it would be better—

And her patience was rewarded. The two men got together through their work. One evening, as Jared was leaving the hospital, an ambulance case came that called for Joel's particular ability to handle frightened, fighting patients.

Standing back, ready to help if needed, Jared watched the skill with which Joel worked, subduing the frightened, injured man, and getting him into the emergency room, on the table, ready to be examined.

"You're as strong as a bull," Jared told Joel when the patient was handed over to the surgeons, who would do what Joel told them.

"I think I've unscrambled his head," said Dr. Joel.

"Will you need further help?"

The eye and ear men thought they could manage. They looked curiously at the two Dr. O'Briens.

Joel went to change his soiled and torn garments. Jared followed him. "You literally have to fight for your job," he said.

Joel grinned. "That chap could have been blinded if he hadn't been settled down. Got in the wrong fight in the first place."

"Yes, he must have. Look. Have you plans for this evening? I don't even know if you're married and have a family. Not even what your hours are here."

Joel wielded a towel. "Not married. No plans. What about you?"

"I thought you might like to ride out with me to our place on the river, and have dinner with my mother and me."

"I'd like that fine. How about your mother?"

"I am the world's worst-spoiled child. And I just happen to know that Zenobia is having chicken and dumplings."

Joel's bright eyes peered above the towel. "Zenobia?"

Jared laughed. "Cook. Housekeeper. Boss of the family."

"Suppose you call her. If it's all right, I'll be with you."

"Fine, fine. We'll go out in my car. And Ivory will drive you back. Ivory, since you are about to ask, is Zenobia's son, and does the outdoor and heavy work about the place."

Joel nodded. "I didn't wear my Sunday suit to work this morning."

"I didn't either," said Jared. "No need."

Helen saw them drive in; she saw them come down the drive, stop to look up at the House. Joel was a bit taller than Jared, his hair a darker blond parted on the side. It blew in the wind. He wore light trousers, a brown jacket and he was laughing.

Jared's blond hair was, as always, smoothly brushed back from his forehead; he was wearing a suit—vest and all—of a dull blue. The sun glinted on the patch on his cheek. He gestured as he talked.

"They like each other," she told Zenobia.

"They fine young men."

"They seem to be."

They were. Jared kissed his mother, and Joel followed suit. "Oh, yes," he said. He knew Jared's mother.

"He's to call me Helen," said that pretty woman, hooking an arm within the elbow of each young man, leading them into the house.

Joel stopped short at the sight of the great bowl of flowers on the table in the hall. He loosed Helen's hand, and went into the first parlor, then the second. Entranced, he stood looking up at the cherubs painted on the ceiling of the east parlor. He went into the living room, and finally the dining room.

"I've never," he said softly, "I have *never* been in a house like this."

Helen and Jared laughed. "Don't miss the hot-water heat radiators," his host advised.

"Well, yes, I've seen them, too. But—what do you call a ceiling like that?"

"Coffered," said Jared. "Here, give me your jacket. It's dinnertime, and we don't dress for dinner."

The ceiling lights twinkled and sparkled from the smoked-glass tabletop. The dinner was delicious, the chicken and dumplings as comfortable in that great room as were the two gold-painted heating coils in the corners. The three people talked steadily—not always waiting on the others for a chance to speak.

The salad was fruit—sweet Anjou pears, white grapes, crisp lettuce. And no dessert.

The talk was selective. Vietnam, briefly. The way the House had been built and purchased. The changes that had been made, those that would never be.

Finished with dinner, they went out to the porch for the sunset. Ivory brought a light shawl for Helen, the jackets for the men. "Do you smoke, sir?" he asked Joel.

Joel shook his head. He was watching a woman who was riding down the river path toward them; she made a glowing picture of life and happiness. Her sorrel was a beautiful animal with long galloping strides.

"Lutie," said Jared, waving to her. She was a pretty woman, with a flashing smile. "She lives next door."

"Lutie?" asked Joel.

"Lucy Reeves," said Helen. "Her father, a widower,

owns the farm north of us. She and Jared grew up together. He couldn't say 'Lucy' when he was three, so she's been Lutie ever since."

"In a properly written book, they now—"

"She married while I was in Nam," said Jared shortly. "Has a little girl."

"She looks so young. Too bad she didn't wait for you."

"Jared told her not to," said Helen quietly.

A glance at Jared told the rest of the story. His face—

"Too bad," Joel said aloud. "It would have been so convenient to have your in-laws next door."

"She thought," offered Helen, "that Jared had found a girl over there. A nurse perhaps."

"Mother—" Jared started to protest, but he was interrupted by the buzz of his beeper. He went into the house to the telephone.

"Were they planning to marry?" Joel asked Helen.

"I think they might have done so. Both were very young."

"Does Jared still think—"

"He does."

"But that's wrong. Is the scar so bad?"

"I've never seen it."

"You—" Joel was shocked.

"He may, some time, of his own accord, wisdom, or need, change his mind about marriage. Meanwhile—"

"You sacrifice your life."

Helen flushed and looked almost angry. "It is no sacrifice," she said, "that I have my son with me."

Joel was still apologizing when Jared came out. "If you're ready to leave," he said, "I think I'll have to go in. Or Ivory can drive you later in Helen's car."

Joel stood up. "I'll go now. Where did I leave my coat?"

She kissed him. "Come again." Then she whispered, "Don't argue the point with him."

"I promise. Good night, Helen."

Jared was puzzled. He himself had invited Joel to the house, he had enjoyed his short time with him. The man had certainly not come mooching for friendship. Jared wondered if he ever would have made the first move. But within that short time he had worked smoothly into the family relationship.

"Where do you live, Joel?" he asked as they neared the hospital.

"In quarters."

"Oh, you can't mean that."

"I do. And it really isn't too bad. Though I plan to find a self-operating apartment."

Jared smiled at the term. "That means one of the hotels, doesn't it?"

"Yes. I was waiting to see what I could afford."

"And today you were named head of traumatic emergency."

"Of course you would know that. But you didn't—"

"I didn't. I understand you are excellent at the job."

"I did an awful lot of it in the Far East. They kept me on for a time."

"And then—"

"I had saved enough to take my time, look around. Your hospital asked me to come see them."

"I didn't have anything to do with that, either."

"I know you didn't. But of course I knew about you."

"Well, I've worked at it longer, and I had the background of a home and family. I just happen to be good at the micro stuff."

Joel only smiled. He knew, and Jared supposed he

knew, that one did not "just happen" to be good at the "stuff" Jared mentioned.

"What do you have tonight?"

"I hope it's a kidney. I have a man who is about to blow the works if he doesn't get a transplant soon. He hates the dialysis bit."

"So would I."

"It was a great discovery."

Joel said nothing. He knew how great it was, but still he would hate it. "In a way," he said musingly, shocked even as he spoke that he did speak, "in a way it's like your face scar. I hate any mutilation."

Jared made no comment. Between the two doctors, the subject would surely come up again. And again. He swung his car into his parking space, and Joel got out on the far side.

"Lock it," said Jared. "I don't want the car messed up."

Joel obeyed. He spoke like a brother, he thought. He could have pitched me out.

Without permission, and without objection either, he followed the older man into the hospital, checked in beside him, and again followed him along the hall. They would, possibly, do a transplant. A donor had been found. A young girl, killed in a traffic accident. The patient had been told and was being prepared.

"If you're tired, good night," Jared said over his shoulder. "But if you'd like to scrub, do. We might use you."

Joel scrubbed and stayed through the transplant. He invited Jared to sleep in quarters. "You're a bit tired to make the drive home."

Jared was shucking out of his O.R. clothes. "I'll go home," he said. "I'm always keyed up, not sleepy, after one of these."

31

Joel nodded. "I would be, too, I guess. Well, thanks for a fine evening and night. I am proud to know I am your brother. Half, as good as you are, is better than being twins."

Jared laughed at his jumbled metaphor, slapped Joel's shoulder and went down to recovery. He must make his orders strong that the patient, a man, must not be told that he would be, Jared hoped, living with a young girl's kidney. Men were often silly about those little things. He could remember a chap who would not stay in the hospital because it was crowded and the only bed for him was in the maternity ward. Men could be damned foolish about some things, and of course mistaken.

He stopped short and looked back along the corridor where Joel was about to turn the corner. He rubbed his tongue along his teeth. What remark would Joel have made to his thoughts? Or Helen? Or—Lutie?

Lutie.

Wide awake, he drove home carefully, and went to bed. He knew that Helen came up to look at him, but he did not move.

Joel was aware, and he suspected that Jared was, how careful he, the younger man, was not to impose his person, his relationship, on Helen and Jared. He had no claim on them. It was Jared who had made the first contact, but he must never be sorry that he had. He kept in touch. Or was it Jared who kept in touch?

The man was busy. He had a definite number of lectures and demonstrations to give for the medical school. His classes were always full. Joel found himself, and saw the students, moving their own fingers to see if they could handle the tiny instruments so deftly, so precisely.

"I feel as if I should wear magnifying glasses," said Joel

half aloud one day. The man next to him nodded. He had been thinking the same thing.

Jared was popular in the sense that everyone, almost, admired him, his work, even his appearance. "When he turns so you can't see that patch, he's handsome," a nurse told Joel.

"Don't you forget it?"

"The patch? Well, yes. But it seems a shame."

Jared was handsome. Slim in his white lab coat, his hair always carefully brushed. He seemed to forget the patch. His fingers never went to his cheek as he lectured; only the students on the benches for the first time thought about it. If a visitor asked about it, his neighbor would say, "Vietnam, piece of mortar shell. I understand it went right through his cheek, his teeth on that side of the face are all replacements."

"Too bad."

"It doesn't seem to bother him."

"I'll bet it does, just the same."

Joel went frequently to the House. Sometimes by special invitation, sometimes on impulse. He too was lonely, for he made few friends in the new location. He had not tried. If Jared was inclined to go up to his desk immediately after dinner, Joel would visit with Helen, or with Brig—a frequent visitor—or content himself with a book to read, a walk to take. He knew that Jared was working on a textbook, reading proof on it, actually.

"He says it is dull. I offered to read for him," said Helen.

"Should I?"

"It might help. He likes you."

How would Joel know? Jared was friendly, but not warm enough for Joel to risk a rebuff. But he was ready to help if he could. And he did offer.

"Find me a new title," said Jared.

"I'd have to know the present one. I realize it is one of these magnificent love stories that are so popular now. Handsome, brave men, sweet, pretty, unawakened women."

"Do you read them?" Helen asked, surprised.

"Only the titles and I hear the blurbs on TV."

"In my youth there was a run of them. My father told us girls not to read them. I obeyed, my sisters did not. They were bound in red, and the author called herself—maybe it was a him—but she called herself 'The Duchess.'"

The men laughed. "I can't use a pen name," said Jared ruefully. "But I'm serious. I do need a title."

"What are you calling it now?" asked Joel.

"I think it's pretty exciting." He glanced at Helen, his eyes twinkling. "*Microsurgery*," he said. "*A Practical Guide for Gynecologists, Urologists, Plastic Surgeons, Neurosurgeons, and Orthopedists.*"

Helen laughed and picked up the evening paper. Joel stared at the serious-faced doctor in the doorway. "It will be thick?" he asked.

Jared measured four inches with his fingers. "And cost thirty bucks," he assured Joel.

"Then I think you should shorten the title," said Joel seriously.

"How?"

"Hmmmnnn, let me see. I believe I'd omit the Micro-surgery."

They all laughed at that, and Jared went upstairs.

"I'm going to take Helen to the movies," Joel called after him.

"Don't eat too much popcorn," Jared called from the landing.

Joel often took Helen places. To a preshow at the Art Museum, to the Shriners' Circus, and tonight to the movies. It rained hard and they came home early. "You'd better stay," Helen told him. "I had a phone put into the brown guest room."

Joel thanked her. Before this he had used a small bedroom on the third floor. The brown guest room was a pleasant place with a braided rug underfoot, a dark, yet bright brown bedspread, a deep chair. Zenobia had stocked the bath with shaving and tooth creams, a clean shirt for the morning. Gradually Joel's own possessions had accumulated.

That night he kissed Helen, and said he was going up to help old Jared.

"Oh, I don't believe I would, dear. He's still working. I saw the light when we drove in."

So had Joel. "I'll make him go to bed. If he had twin beds up there, I'd stay and see that he did."

Helen watched him get his medical bag out of his car and go up the stairs. Jared never left his bag in the car either. Were doctors made of one sort?

She was tempted to tiptoe upstairs and eavesdrop on the men. Would Jared be polite or order Joel out? What would be Joel's approach? She herself never "bothered" Jared when he was working.

But Joel approached, unafraid. He heard Jared in the shower. On his worktable was a neatly boxed package. "You found a name?" he asked when Jared came out, wielding a mighty towel.

"Sure did. Spent half an hour deciding between *Microsurgery, A Guide* or—"

Joel laughed. "Or *A Guide to Microsurgery*."

"I'm going to bed."

"So am I. I've been made a patient in the brown guest room."

"Officially?"

"Officially. It's raining mangy dogs and scabby kittens out. I clocked in on my own telephone." Joel opened his bag on the table.

Jared frowned. "What goes on?"

"I'm earning my keep. Sit down. I'll dress your cheek."

"Like hell you will."

"Like an experienced doctor, I will. If it means a fight, Helen will hear you hit the floor."

Jared was helpless. "I dress my own cheek," he grumbled.

"A second opinion is advised."

Jared grumbled. He never—for years no one had seen or "dressed" his cheek. But eventually he sat down in the chair. Joel took the green shade off the table light, and slipped into thin gloves. "I wouldn't want to catch what you've got," he explained.

This remark was so unexpected that Jared laughed, even as he clutched at the patch which Joel had swiftly ripped away. "Oh, dear," he said softly. Skin had never grown completely over the nasty triangular scar. Deep, angry still . . .

He turned to take a small jar from his bag.

With deft hands, cotton, soothing lotions, he cleaned the whole cheek area. He considered the scar itself, took scissors from a plastic bag and cut away a tag of dry flesh. "It's hard to be tidy when you get one of these where you can't debride with your own best hand," he murmured. "God, man, you must have had a nasty face."

"I did. And it lay in the mud for a day and a half. I had other injuries. My back. Compact humerus. I had the choice of swallowing blood or lying in it when I spit it out."

Joel grunted. "Nam didn't run much to antisepsis," he agreed. "But I'm glad you were found."

"My sergeant did that. And the burial platoon."

"And they took you to the hospital."

"After they'd turned me over, so I had to swallow the blood."

Joel made grunting, grieving sounds. "That's why you hate the thing so much."

"Of course. I could guess what I looked like. It was the chaplain who persuaded me to be glad my eye had escaped."

"I'm glad, too. How long . . . ?"

"Two years. I wouldn't let Helen be told until I could talk to her myself. And I wouldn't let her come to see me until I had teeth and a bandage that covered my face and head. By then my arm and back were in good shape."

"She must have gone through her own little hell."

"Not little. But I knew she couldn't imagine what I looked like. The bruises alone . . ."

Joel's hands were gentle and deft. Jared wouldn't look at his face.

"But she knew that you were wounded . . ."

"Just the arm. Of course I sent word to Lutie—"

"And she thought you'd met a nurse."

Jared shrugged, and Joel's hand quickly stilled any movement of his head. He had filled the cavity with a soothing cream, and now was carefully removing the thick of it.

"If she loved you," Joel said, "as you knew your mother did . . ." He spoke thoughtfully.

"Being married to a girl is different," said Jared angrily.

"Yes," Joel agreed.

"All I had left was my profession," said Jared, still angry. "I did a lot of concentrating on my skill with my fingers."

"You had other things," Joel insisted.

37

"A face whose touch, whose sight, would be repulsive to any woman."

"Not to your mother."

"I don't know," said Jared. "I have never put her to the test."

"Of course not," said Joel dryly. Deftly he had cleaned the cheek. "The scar looks more peaceful," he told Jared.

"It feels that way, too. You knew what you were doing."

"This is a trauma if I ever saw one."

Jared accepted the explanation.

"I feel a small lecture coming on," Joel said quietly.

"I've composed and listened to them all."

"Lutie is a very fine young woman."

Jared said nothing.

"And you cheated her of your children. Just as you cheated Helen of her grands."

Jared looked up, then accepted the term. "It hasn't been easy on me," he said grimly.

"Helen handles it better than you do."

"Yes. She's found ways of living with people. Except for the hospital, I can't take the questions. Especially the unspoken ones.

Joel picked up a fresh patch and began to fit it smoothly into place.

"It wasn't easy to take up surgery again," said Jared grumpily. "I wanted to stay in the lab, develop instruments."

"But there would come along a case . . ."

Jared's silence agreed with him. "I lecture," he defended himself. "And teach."

"I wish Helen had married again."

"She could have. Men like her."

"Why not? Beautiful, and with a character— Don't *you* ever think of marrying?"

"In Nam I did. Not after I came home and realized the look of horror my face would bring. I couldn't take that, Joel."

"I suppose you couldn't." Joel was cleaning up his gear.

"Just let the thing alone, will you?" Jared asked angrily.

"O.K. If that's what you want."

He took his bag and left the room. It seemed strangely empty without him. Jared softly touched his cheek. He had given Joel small thanks for what he had done. His face felt better than it ever did after his own dressing. As for his "lecture"—well, Jared had heard all those things in his own conscience. He gave his wrapped manuscript a push, put the green shade back on the lamp, and went to bed. The rain had stopped.

He couldn't get to sleep. The trees dripped, small noises sounded sharp. He thought of what he had said about Helen, and her marrying again. Joel must remember their father better than Jared did. Much, much better. Things he had read and been told about the bishop— Why had Helen married him in the first place? She was an ardent church worker, and the idea of a young priest falling in love with her had entranced the young girl. That was Jared's explanation. A time or two he had questioned his mother; once he had spoken to an aunt. "He was a difficult man," they all said.

So was Jared, his son. From things he had said to Joel that night. As for Lutie. . . . He turned in bed so that the moonlight struck the square package on the table. His book. Meant to be a textbook. It would be read and believed. Which was all right. He had done the thing thoughtfully, meaning to be helpful.

He had told the presumably young surgeon who would read it that it was nonsense to say a microsurgeon should never have a drink of coffee, or have a snort of liquor. "You will be able to gauge the strength and reliability of your hands," he wrote. "Some of you may like to operate from a chair, possibly with arm rests; some of you may not be able to survive a vacation, a week, without doing microsurgery. Different men need and do different things."

Which was what he had tried to tell Joel about his marrying Lutie.

"You'll develop your own dogmas about this work," he remembered writing. "They won't be mine or your teacher's. But when you have made your rules, established the things that help you do the best work, don't try to enforce your methods on any newcomers. Be yourself. Learn to keep your hand steady, learn to see and to value the tiniest thing—or give up microsurgery. Let it be as simple as that."

So Jared had learned. In the military hospital where he had convalesced, wise staffmen had let him work on the thing that interested him. He was given a small laboratory space and had experimented with the breeding of twin mice, and then had practiced transplants on them.

"We may not develop a genius," a staff doctor had said, "but I'm pretty sure we'll keep this one sane. If he can keep busy." And so Jared had learned microprocedure by himself. He experimented with organ transplants on rats, all the time hoping to develop his microsurgical skills so that he could research human organ transplants, especially kidneys. The microsurgery for fertility came later, but he was as of that day doing less and less kidney work.

He taught himself, and did anything to compensate for his face and what it was costing him. He was always glad of a chance to teach new would-be microsurgeons. He developed little tricks and stunts to perform during a lecture.

His hands, he declared, were no steadier than those of the average surgeon. To prove this, or try to, he would take up a nylon suture, thread a tiny needle, pick it up with tweezers, and make stitching motions. The right hand did actually waver just a bit. But he declared that with concentration and the high magnification he used in the operating rooms, his hands were as steady as rocks. "It's all in your head," he declared. "Concentration. Not in your hands."

But his powers of concentration were such that when he indulged in a hobby he had of photographing wild animals using his 500 mm lens, he did not use a tripod, a procedure few professionals would dare to neglect.

Thinking of these things his eyes drooped, and he drifted to sleep. Again his profession had soothed away the hurt of Lutie. He called it compensation for his face. But that compensation was not complete.

He still could not live socially. He would go into the city to see a good play, or the Symphony if it had an alluring program. But dinner parties, big weddings, what he called *soirées*, were not possible. Or, he decided, necessary.

But there was one thing—

"I should think it would be difficult," said Joel, ignoring Helen's head-shake of warning, "to get up in church and conduct a service, preach a sermon."

"I face a class of students," said Jared. "I address a convocation of medics. In the same spirit, I can do a lay reader service."

And he did. When he was in the hospital so long, having plastic surgery, he and the chaplain had become great friends. Jared would go to the chaplain's office, and read the "stuff" on his desk. In the hospital, no one noticed scars.

41

And at the chaplain's gentle suggestion, he studied for and got his license as a lay reader in the church. Somehow to put on the vestments, go through the beautiful service, was a right thing to do. He would read the sermon, and read it well. When permission was given, he composed his own sermons, liking to research and write them. His voice was good. To go into a tiny church, or to mount the pulpit of a large one, he became a different man.

His mother was happy when she learned what he was doing. The aunts began to brag about it, but Jared himself stopped that. "This is not a circus," he told them. "I could do the same duty in my hospital whites."

Joel agreed that he could, and said nothing to discourage this strange brother of his. No one ever said a thing about his being like his father.

He was his own man, and the bishop had had no influence on him.

"Except for genes," Jared reminded him.

"You gotta watch them things," agreed Joel, reaching his racket to catch the ball sailing toward him.

Up on the verandah, Helen and her sisters watched the two men play with rackets and a white ball on the green grass.

They did not look alike, and yet they were alike. They knew by some instinct what to do, and when. They squabbled, yet they knew moments of showing true affection for each other. And always love for Helen. "They are nice boys," she told Zenobia, and her sisters, and Lutie.

His patients recognized the quality in Jared. Men would come to him, not wanting to come, and return gladly. "I believe he can do it," they would say.

The students watched each of them. "How do you learn

to be the way those two are," one young man asked his advisor. "They look like any man in a white coat, and yet—"

"Learn your job," said the older person. "See the trust we all have in Dr. Jared, the *envy* we have—that's the only word I can find to describe our admiration for him."

Now and then one of their contemporaries would ask Joel, "How did you get in with lily fingers?"

Joel hated the term, though he respected Jared's talents and skill. "I was born to it," he said.

"Closed corporation, huh?"

"That's right."

"You're rougher and tougher."

"Don't put it to a try."

"You ever try it?"

"Not me. I'm the smart O'Brien."

This made it a joke, enough so that the other doctor would accept the answer.

His mother knew that it was an answer. Now, watching them race and turn, twist and run against the green grass, she would nod to her companion.

"Why don't they marry?" asked Charlotte. The sisters— the "aunties" had come for dinner.

"I don't know."

"Don't you ask them?"

"When Joel first came to us, I asked him. His reply was another question. 'What about Jared?'"

"Did Joel give you any answer but that?"

"Yes."

Charlotte waited.

"Just once," said Helen.

The two older women leaned forward.

Helen laughed at the intensity of their interest.

43

"You don't want Jared to marry," accused Adelaide.

"With a compromise," said Helen after a pause. "Joel told me he would marry if and when Jared did."

"That wasn't much of an answer."

"It was all I got, though he acknowledged that it was a compromise."

"Would he do it?"

"I don't know. Men make their choices. Joel said that he would stay and help the project along."

"Lutie is free, and living with her father."

"Yes."

"What happens if Joel takes her away from Jared?"

"He might." Helen clutched at her serenity.

There were times when Helen herself wondered about Joel. Jared probably did, as well. He and the young woman had taken up their teenage friendship with each other. The baby, a little girl, was a "doll," and took his infrequent word of discipline in the right spirit. No doubt because of Lutie's supervision and advice. She was, as all children, more frank than her elders. She asked outright about the silver patch on Jared's cheek. Helen and Lutie and Joel breathlessly awaited his reply.

"I got a hurt-you," Jared answered readily.

"Do you have to keep it wrapped up?"

"No."

For Maggie's age, that was answer enough. But one evening later, the matter came up again when he and Joel were walking Lutie and the child home after supper. And she asked again about the patch.

"What sort of hurt-you?" she asked. "Does it have a name?"

"Yes," said Jared. "You couldn't spell it."

"Can you say it?"

"Doctors use big words," Jared warned.

Lutie's blue eyes waited on his answer.

Jared stood thoughtful. "You know that I am a doctor."

Of course she knew. And that Joel was one, also. "Well," said Jared, "could you remember or care about a transurethral prostatic resection?"

Joel snorted. "I don't think that's what you have," said Lutie. "But it must be bad or you'd give her the right name. I just think you have a hole or a blister in your cheek."

"You come closer than I did," Jared assured her.

"And you're tired in the evenings."

"Sometimes."

"Can you spell those words?" asked Lutie.

"Not unless I have to," said Jared. He had worked all afternoon on the surgery he had named. But he'd saved the man; he would be a functioning husband.

"Do you think," Joel asked Helen after Jared had gone to drive the aunties home, "that Jared would marry if I do?"

She looked up at him in alarm. "Now, don't you . . . "

"I won't. I won't," said Joel quickly. "Lutie would say 'yes' and that would end things."

"I don't think Jared would marry," said Jared's mother.

"Then I'll stay around and help. Because he should."

Helen said nothing. And after a bit Joel asked, "Do I help?"

"You help enormously. I think you know that."

Joel had no reply. If only because his regular dressing of Jared's "hurt-you" was gradually closing the terrible hole. Jared could have done it himself, or gone to some doctor

45

who would have done it. The point was he had done little except prevent infection.

"He would not have treated a patient so," said Helen. "But you have a life of your own. It's not right for one man to dictate to another."

The bishop had assumed that right. "I think," Joel said gently "that the decision is mine, not yours or Jared's."

He was right. She believed that Joel should make such a decision when the time came. But if the move should be to Lutie, there could be real tragedy. She knew, even if Jared did not, that her son still loved Lutie.

"Well," she said, picking up her book, "at least now Jared has someone to talk to."

"He's popular at the hospital."

"Liked?"

Joel puzzled over that. "Admired, of course."

"But does he have friends?"

Joel frowned. "He scarcely has time, Helen."

She nodded. "I suppose he doesn't have time for much of that."

"There's the head nurse on his service."

"Yes. I know. But even she is a little in awe of him. You're not. That's what you give him."

"Others give him liking that is more than admiration. There's this baby. Maybe he's talked about her. Some doctor in a smaller medical area had bungled the treatment."

"The vestigial kidney?"

"That's the one. Jared's working like hell to get the child in a condition where she can hope to marry some day. As it is, she wears a diaper, and the prospect is she always will. That's no future for a young girl growing up. In a way he compounds her case with his own injury. He could marry, but already he's thinking of the man she could love eighteen years from now and want to marry."

"Women handle such things."

"Men don't, always. But maybe Jared will find a way— he's very tender with the child. The same as he is with Lutie's little girl. He loves children and should have some of his own."

Helen sighed. "And we can't talk about it."

"No. We cannot."

3

Gradually, almost without notice, Joel began escorting Helen to places she wanted to go, or needed to go, at night. Jared had been doing this when he was able. One evening at dinner, Helen made them all laugh at her tales of being "stood up" by her date. "You can tell if it's a bad play," she said. "Jared's home at five, and off we go. But if the phone rings at six with the message that he will be detained, I don't have to read the reviews next day. The play was a smash."

They laughed, even Ivory, who was serving.

Helen glanced up at him as she sat back to let him put her slice of roast on her plate. "I could go alone," she admitted. "I have a dozen friends who would like to go with me."

"Instead you sit here and— What is it you do, Mum?"

Joel's head lifted. "Don't you know?"

"Sometimes," said Helen serenely, "I just stay at home. And I take comfort in the thought that I shan't have to buy a new dress for the next affair. I save money that way."

They laughed and went on with their dinner. But gradually, if Jared were detained at the hospital, Joel would appear, dressed to accompany Helen. "Did Jared ask you to do this?" she asked him on one occasion.

"No. But I knew that he had called you."

"How . . . ?"

"You ask too many questions. But the truth is, I like beating his time."

"What will people think?"

"That I am Jared."

"No, they won't. You two don't look that much alike."

But there were errors made. A woman said to Helen that she had thought her son was blonder. Another—a man— said the same thing and this made Helen and Joel laugh, but Jared was furious when told about it. "If people would only listen to introductions!" he growled. "They don't, any more than they read the instructions I give them."

"When I was younger," said Helen serenely, but with laughter sparkling in her eyes, "I had some minor surgery and the doctor gave me a typed sheet of what I should and should not do after I reached home."

"I have those instructions printed and given to every patient," Jared informed her.

"And they put them on the car seat where they can blow out the window."

"No doubt," said Jared. "And something of that sort may have happened in this case I had today."

"What about him, dear?" Helen urged, hoping to prolong the conversation.

"Well, actually nothing," said Jared. "To him or to his wife, except that she came to me yesterday, absolutely furious because she had been examined and tested, and what was she to do about it? She was four months pregnant."

"I'd say she should wait five months," murmured Joel.

"Didn't she want the child?" asked Helen.

"I gathered that neither she nor her husband wanted one. They already had two, and he had—after a good deal of thought—he had decided to have a vasectomy. Some idiot had told him I was the best in that line."

"But aren't you?"

"Evidently not. Because he had the surgery—"

"And she's four months pregnant."

"Could be the fellow down the street," suggested Joel.

"I didn't think about that," said Jared. "Instead, in my usual bungling way, I asked her to have her husband drop in to see me. I even made the appointment for him."

"And he came?" asked Joel, his face and eyes innocent.

Jared nodded. "He came," he agreed. "In a rush, in a rage, both of which were multiplied about ten times because he had to wait until I got out of surgery. A half hour or so. And everybody on the fourth floor found a reason to come in and send me word to slide down the drainpipe."

"But you didn't," murmured Helen.

"I took my time changing. I don't like angry post-ops."

"You knew that that was what he was?"

"Yes. His wife—I had done a vasectomy on her husband—"

"I can quote what he said," offered Joel.

"Not with Mother present," Jared warned. Joel nodded and settled back in his chair.

"He was about the maddest I've had," said Jared. "Even told me to go back to medical school, and he asked where I'd got my reputation for being a hotshot surgeon. I don't think I've seen a patient any madder."

"Do you get a lot like that, dear?" asked Helen.

"About one a year."

"I still think you're a hotshot surgeon."

50

Joel laughed. "He is, dear," he said. "He is. Your loyalty is warranted. And the man had wasted the hotshot's whole morning."

"Oh, not quite," said Jared. "I asked to see the instruction sheet I had given him when he left the hospital."

"And he said, of course, that he didn't have it."

"That is exactly what he said, But when I asked if he had ever read it, he said he thought he had. But things seemed all right, and he was a busy man, and—"

"He'd had the flu," murmured Joel. "The usual excuse for not following instructions."

Jared glanced at him. "Yes, of course he said that, and that he'd had to go out of town. He'd meant to come back for me to see if things were all right."

"And that he didn't need to come back to let the doctor see if things had gone all right."

"That's what he said," agreed Jared. "Then he asked me if many of my vasectomies failed. I told him one did, occasionally. And he asked what I was going to do about it."

Joel leaned forward, "And you said that you would test him, but that it could be the man in the next apartment."

"Joel," Helen reproved him.

"He was being pretty rough on our boy."

"I'm used to it," said Jared. "I told him he had taken a foolish chance not to return for a checkup."

"This won't affect the child, will it?" asked Helen.

"I sincerely hope not. The fellow has four or five months to get used to the idea."

"And did you tell him you would reverse the procedure so he'd know he could have more children?"

Jared gaped at Joel. "You've been talking to Lutie," he said accusingly.

"Is there any reason why I shouldn't talk to Lutie?"

51

"None at all," said Jared, touching his napkin to his lips, and rising. "Excuse me, Mum?" he asked. "I've some notes to get in shape. I do a lecture demonstration in Boston this weekend."

"Did I say too many wrong things?" Joel asked Helen when he resumed his chair.

"One has to know Jared," Helen reminded him.

"I admire him tremendously."

"I know you do. And he probably does have notes to get in order if he's to demonstrate his procedure to restoring a man's ability to fertilize a woman."

"Have you seen him do that?"

"I've never seen Jared operate."

"You should sometime. But the way he threads thick yarn into your small needles is a good example. It adds an hour or two to the process, but he delicately cuts out the sections of any damaged tubes—I think he is the only doctor doing the procedure and he has received much attention for it."

"Lutie knows he is often asked to present papers on it," said Helen.

"She told me. But she doesn't really like to talk about Jared and his work."

"Those kids were badly hurt by her marriage."

"Yes. One evening, we were wading in the river. Trying to catch frogs with our toes."

"Three years old," laughed Helen.

"At least that. And she got to musing about old Jared."

"What did she say?" Helen turned the spoons beside her plate end for end. "About Jared? Sometimes I think she is still in love with him."

"She knows him better than I do. And she spoke calmly, almost as if she had been his wife, lived with him for many years. What kind of guy was she married to?"

"Let's talk about Jared. While she was married she lived in Philadelphia and would come home for short vacations. So . . ."

Joel nodded. "Let me see. She said he liked individuals rather than people in a group. He liked to plan things ahead."

"Oh, yes," breathed his mother. And waited. Ivory came to the pantry door and she shook her head at him.

Joel resumed. "Jared dislikes surprises. I've found that out for myself. He hates interruptions in something he's planned. He values his own privacy and maybe he respects the privacy of others too much. When I first knew him I thought he was cold and standoffish."

Helen shook her head. "He is devoted but not effusive."

"Yes. Lutie said something like that. She also said he was a little shy."

"He is."

"But that surprises me. He has fine manners to everyone usually. And he dresses meticulously, but one day when an exceedingly Big Wig was going to endow a new wing or tower or something expensive, and the staff was asked to arrange to attend the meeting, Jared came in late, in his scrub suit and a stained one at that. He pulled a chair up to the corner of the table instead of taking the place left open for him with the staff. He left early without saying the few things he was down on the schedule to say."

Helen looked shocked, "What . . .?"

"I am sure you know the way he goes up to his rooms or down by the river, and doesn't want anyone to join him. He is thinking something out, or maybe trying not to think."

"He seems to have an imperative need for times of silence and solitude."

"Has he been this way all his life?"

"No. Just since he was injured in Vietnam and spent so much time in the hospital. I am sure he is grateful for what help you have been to him."

"He could have done it for himself."

Helen looked surprised. "Why didn't he?"

"I asked him. Just once."

"And got no answer."

"For one thing," Joel continued, "he acknowledges boundaries and keeps within them better than anyone I've ever known. In the hospital, in his personal relationships. With you, with me. And he never trespasses. . . . Lutie says he's a crank." He said this after a pause of reflection.

Helen looked up in surprise. "But, yes, he is. Sometimes, Do you talk about Jared to Lutie?"

"Oh, yes. He's still in love with the girl."

"I know," sighed Helen.

"I told her to seduce him."

Helen's eyes flew wide. "You didn't!"

"I certainly did. And she was shocked, too. But I told her to do it."

"He thinks she married the man she did because she didn't love Jared. He didn't send us word, you know— We didn't get word of him for months and months."

"But in Nam . . ."

"I know. I waited. She was young—and didn't."

Joel followed her from the dinner table and then tried to find Jared. Had he returned to the hospital? Ivory said his car was in the garage. He wasn't in his rooms. But after dark he came up to the house, carrying his shoes. "I was down by the river," he said tersely. "Were you looking for me?"

"I don't like to be alone as much as you do."

Jared set his shoes aside. "Were you looking for me?"

"As I said, I don't like to be alone as much as you do."

Jared began to undress. "Can you write a sermon?" he asked unexpectedly.

Joel laughed. "Not me. Can you?"

"I have to preach one tomorrow."

"Our father had books and books of sermons."

Jared turned on the shower. "Did you go to church?"

"I had to when he was around. I never went when he was gone. And don't say that now you know why I am as I am."

Jared laughed. "I have to preach tomorrow," he said again.

"Lutie told me."

"How does she know?"

"I thought maybe you'd told her."

"I don't see a great deal of Lutie."

"Why not? You like her."

Jared said nothing.

"I'll dress your face. You'll want to look handsome."

Jared grunted.

"Do you write your own sermons?"

"No. If I get beeped, you can preach for me."

"Not me. I'll answer your beep."

"That might be less disastrous."

But the next morning, his surprise shown only by a lifted eyebrow, Jared saw his mother, Joel, and Lutie sitting in a front side pew of the old, small church. They had come especially to hear him serve as lay reader. Joel found himself listening as he had never listened to the sermons of his father, the bishop. Both Lutie and Helen noted his intent face.

"They are alike," Lutie whispered to Helen, who put her hand on the younger woman's wrist. ". . . We'll get scolded . . . ," Helen whispered.

Lutie sat back in the pew. "I heard him rehearsing it down by the river last night," she said. "He didn't see me. He was so absorbed, he almost walked right into the water."

Helen's pressure on her wrist became heavier. And Lutie was silent, her pretty face uplifted to the man in white who stood above them.

"A person may best judge himself," Jared was saying, his voice rich and deep, "and be judged by the enemies he has.

"If one has definite opinions, if one has fixed standards, and lives by them, declares them, there will be those made uncomfortable. *Unhappy* is the term. And naturally, it seems, opposition results. He may not be liked.

"Of course if one lives less than by the moral code, again he may be judged by those who disagree with him. By the law, regulated society and so on, you don't expect this. But do not grieve if the dull, the fuzzy thinkers, the petty, do not 'like' you. Would you change to ways they would like?"

"I'm proud of him," Lutie told Helen as they walked out of church. "And I kept remembering the awful song he and I composed when he was a Boy Scout."

"Jared composed a song?" Joel asked in surprise.

"He did the lyrics, and they were worse than my bad music. Let me see. The title was *I Found a Peach in Orange, New Jersey.*"

Joel laughed and Helen shook her head. "You should come out of a church service with nobler thoughts," she told Lutie.

The pretty young woman laughed. "But it was no worse than what is being sung on TV now."

"Scant praise, scant praise," said Joel, opening the car door.

56

"I'm going to see if I can find a copy of that song," Lutie said.

"What made you think Jared's sermon . . . ?"

"Because it was so much better," she said serenely. "He's come quite a way."

Frequently, Joel talked to Helen about Jared, and in turn, Lutie talked to her about Joel.

She had begun to have doubts about coming home after she found herself single again. "I should have gotten a job and supported Maggie and me," she said.

"You still can do that. But how would you manage with Maggie?"

Lutie had walked up the path to where Helen was working in her garden. "You have enough to do to raise the child," Helen assured her. "And since your mother died your father is alone. He enjoys having you at home."

"I didn't plan things," said Lutie. "That's always been my trouble."

"You wanted children. You have Maggie." As always Helen spoke quietly.

"I know. Helen, Joel and Jared had the same father."

"That's right."

"But he's no actual blood relative to you."

"He's my stepson."

"Oh, come on, now."

"But he is, Lutie."

"He certainly isn't much like Jared."

"His mother probably was not much like me."

"Didn't you know her?"

"Only pictures in the newspaper when the bishop died."

"Are either of the boys like him?"

"No-o. Jared certainly is not. He even preaches better than his father did."

"And you're no relation? To Joel, I mean."

"I can't see that I am. Why? But I love him like a son. He's been good for our house. He shakes Jared up."

"Yes, he does. I wish Jared were more like him."

"You're still in love with Jared."

"Yes, I am. But he doesn't know it."

"Joel does."

"He says, if it weren't for Jared, he'd try to make love to me."

"Oh, dear. That would make a mess of things."

"Helen, do you think . . . ?"

"I can't think realistically about Jared. I didn't when he was in Vietnam, and we thought he had been killed. To me he was still a blond-haired baby."

"And you don't see him now as a giant in medicine."

"Heavens, no!" Helen laughed.

"But he is one, dear."

"I know it without acknowledging that the giant is my son. I even wish he were more like Joel. Relaxed. Fun to have around. I do love him, Lutie."

"I know. But he thinks only of his scar, his face."

"It doesn't bother me."

"It does me. It's the reason he won't date girls, dance, or marry."

"As if you'd mind."

"I wouldn't. I might advise him to go to a plastic surgeon. Joel is tender with him about it. And Jared lets Joel dress it."

Lutie looked up at the House and tugged at the harness around the wandering baby. And she sighed.

Helen patted her arm. "Get Maggie out of the mud puddle, dear. I wish you had waited for him. Jared, I mean. And that this was my grandchild."

"I did wait for him. When he was found and brought to

the hospital—you were notified—I wrote to him. He didn't answer. You know all that."

"Yes. He wrote only briefly to me. He said he might come home, he might not. And to tell you not to wait for him."

"But I did, for a time. I finished college. I got a job. And George came on the scene. He wasn't Jared, by any means."

"I liked George. Though I was jealous of him."

Lutie sighed. "I did wrong by him. I wouldn't have a child at first. Though I wanted Jared's children. And finally George persuaded me."

"You love Maggie. Why did you divorce George?"

"He got tired of being a ghost in my life. That was his explanation. And I tired of being married to a ghost. I am sure Jared disapproves of me. He used to kiss me like a sister. But he doesn't any more."

"Joel does."

"Yes. Sometimes I wish—"

"Don't do it, Lutie."

Lutie's eyes flew wide. They were green eyes, flecked with gold. "I wouldn't and Joel wouldn't let me. But sometimes, Helen," she drew the baby to her lap and cuddled her, "sometimes I wish Jared were more like Joel. He deliberately came to work with him. You know Joel did."

"Actually . . . "

"I know. They do entirely different work. But they did come together and make a family unit."

"Yes, they did. If Jared would relax his defensive—"

"Mhmnnn. That's what I mean. Let himself forget who he is, what had happened to him. He could be more—more gregarious than he is. Forget his face. He could be more spontaneous and impromptu."

"I don't think this house could take two like Joel. Though I enjoy him."

Lutie laughed. "I know what you mean. He went to the supermarket with me one day, and he turned the buying of a pork chop into a three-ring circus. He adores a crowd."

"Yes. When he takes me to the symphony or even to church, he draws every man, woman and child into his orbit."

"He's wonderful with children. He is imaginative and helpful."

"Good fun," Helen agreed. "And Jared enjoys his nonsense, though he told Joel once that he was overpowering."

Lutie looked shocked. "What did Joel say?"

"He looked thoughtful, then said something about his having limitless charm and vitality. That made Jared laugh, and we went on from there. Have you ever seen him with Jared's aunties?"

Lutie looked up quickly. "What's happened?" She knew Helen's two older sisters who, too often, undertook to advise her or comment on matters that concerned only Helen's home.

Helen began to put her gardening tools away. The sun was getting hot. The baby had fallen asleep. "Let's go up to the porch," she said. "This really takes telling."

"I should take Maggie home for her lunch and a nap."

"I wanted to tell you—"

"I'll come back. If the boys won't be here."

The "boys" were Jared and Joel, and Helen smiled at the term.

"They think I'm chasing Jared," Lutie explained.

"He'd like you to chase him and catch him."

Lutie looked earnestly at Jared's mother. "Would he, really?"

"Not the chasing part, maybe. But he wishes he were married to you. I'm sure he does, Lutie."

"Then why doesn't he do something about it?" asked Lutie, a bit crossly.

"Remember how we started this talk. We agreed that Jared could be shy."

"Oh, for heaven's sake," said Lutie. "No wonder Joel told me to seduce him."

Helen laughed. "Why don't you?"

"Frankly," said the younger woman, "I don't know how."

"You did when you were fifteen."

"Yes, but they went and had a war. He didn't come back the same."

"And you jumped to conclusions. I've always meant to ask. Did he send you word that he had married?"

"No," said Lutie frankly. "He said for me not to wait to marry him. That it couldn't happen."

Helen nodded. "He told me not to come to see him, but I did when he reached the States. Now! Take Maggie up to her grandpa for lunch and her nap. And we'll have our lunch on the porch while I tell you about Joel and my sisters."

"Did they ever have a date, Helen?"

"I don't remember any. Just their club meetings—things like that."

Lutie nodded, and gathered up the child and started for home. Helen watched her go. She worried for fear Joel would step between Jared and Lutie. That simply must not happen! She thought she'd tell the volatile young man so.

Helen's parents had died some years ago. Amanda had married a young lawyer whom they all admired for one reason and another, and had moved to the eastern part of the country, where she had died of an unsuspected cancer

61

and her husband of a heart attack two years later. This left Charlotte and Adelaide with the family home, and a comfortable income. Would Helen and "her boy" come and live there? They had asked this.

Helen had said "No," firmly. She was well content with the bishop's parents, her little son and the House, the expansive acreage, the river and the gardens.

Never again would she "cut paper dolls in the basement." At the House she was loved and a person in her own right.

Then the sisters threatened; they would sell the home, and get a smaller one.

"I think you should," Helen had agreed.

This they had done, not consulting her again, establishing themselves near enough both to the library and the church that they had known all their lives. Adelaide worked part-time in the library. Charlotte was overly active in the church.

"She runs all of us," said the rector. "We do things the wrong way or we do them Charlotte's way."

"And like it?" Helen teased.

"The things have to be done."

"And they get done Charlotte's way. I know."

Helen thought about this while she helped arrange a small table for herself and Lutie. Was she being disloyal to tell about Joel and the sisters? She didn't feel that she was. They no longer seemed to be a part of her family. Was this wrong of her? No. The sisters, like their mother, had never been particularly interested in Helen. She had let them have the home and use such estate as there was. No! She had married, and taken care of Jared. Joel was an additional bonus.

"Joel," she told Lutie when she returned in a fresh blouse and skirt, her blond hair brushed to a sheen, "Joel helped—Well, that was his purpose—though I knew and he knew he was doing less than help the girls."

"I love the way you call them 'the girls,'" said Lutie, who had known the sisters all her life. Two small, plump women, with hair dressed exactly alike. They wore clothes that were good but out of date by two or three years. White gloves always—and hats. Simple felt or straw hats. They possessed none of Helen's beauty, the loveliness she showed in her choice of clothes.

"Was Amanda like you or them?" she asked unexpectedly.

"You knew Amanda."

"Briefly, when she would visit you. I remember she said *to-mah-to* instead of tomato."

"She learned to do that when she moved East. She was striking looking and she had style."

Lutie nodded, and ate some of the rice and tuna fish on her plate.

"They were to give a small dinner," said Helen, continuing her story about the "girls." "They came over here to talk to me about it. Some committee from the National Cathedral was to be there, and they thought the party should not be in the church."

"Why didn't they give it in their house?"

"They didn't want to cook a meal and serve it."

"Nor pay to have it catered."

"I suggested that, but they said there would be the cleaning up to do afterward. You know the kind of house they keep. If they see you lift a paperweight and set it down, they move it to the exact quarter of an inch you have missed."

"Don't ever bring them to see me," sighed Lutie. "How did you manage when Jared was little?"

"I didn't take him there."

Lutie's eyebrows lifted. "Go on," she said.

"Well, Joel was home that evening, but Jared was not. Joel outdid himself being charming to my sisters, and when the problem of the dinner came up he suggested a restaurant."

"And the aunties didn't like cafeterias."

Helen laughed. "They didn't go that far," she said, "but they did say they seldom ate out at night, and so didn't know . . ."

"So Joel offered—"

"He did, and the girls were in a twitter of gratitude and admiration for him; they set no limits as to place, price, food. 'Just have it especially nice and different,' said Adelaide."

"And he did. He said he thought the guests from Washington should see our river—"

"I understand you don't mean our little one here."

"I don't. And I didn't ask any questions."

"Or tell Jared."

"That was an oversight. When I was invited to attend I thought I would go with Joel, but he had a big thing happen at the trauma center, and he told Jared to take me. We each took a car and went where we were told to pick up the guests, including my sisters, and then down to the Equitable Building. Joel assured us that we would be expected."

"Toni's?" Lutie asked warily.

"Yes. Charlotte was prepared to pay the check."

"Wasn't it terribly expensive?"

"It was. But that came later. The guests were charming people, and I was sure that they were used to places like Toni's. They were surprised that there need be no reservations. I told them that I thought Dr. O'Brien had consulted with the maitre d'."

"Had he?"

"Of course. They've remodeled it, you know."

"I've heard. But I don't rate dinners there."

"Don't you have plenty of money, dear?"

"When I visit at home. If I go to work and have to manage the baby and an apartment, I'll have to scrabble."

"Then do as Joel says. Seduce Jared. He makes wads of money, besides what he has from his grandparents."

"I have better reasons for wishing Jared . . ."

Helen's slim fingers touched her hand. "It's a very good reason if you need one," she said. "I've done the scrabbling bit, you know."

"Did you?" Lutie was intensely interested.

"In those days young priests got very little money. Things are better for them now."

"I hope so."

"But higher salaries make things difficult for the small churches."

"Were we talking about Toni's?"

Helen smiled. "Yes, we were. Will you eat some sliced peaches for dessert?"

"Of course. I eat anything."

"Good girl. We must take you to Toni's. Where were we?"

"You said they'd established themselves in the Equitable Building. I've seen that only from the outside. All shining steel that reflects everything."

"It does. The best place to see it is from the revolving roof restaurant across the street."

"I've been there. Now—Toni's. And the sisters' guests. And Joel."

"Yes. Here come our peaches. Thank you, Ivory."

Lutie picked up her spoon, poised it over the pale green glass bowl of beautiful peach slices. And waited.

"The restaurant is as modern as tomorrow's moonshot," said Helen. "One enters through the lobby of the big office building. And I, at least, gasped to find myself in a miniature botanical garden of blooming flowers and greenery. This frames a high sculpture. Charlotte and Adelaide didn't look at it very long but herded their party past the bar. I hung back and got a good look but no drink."

"Episcopalians drink."

"Not when guests of my sisters."

"No, I guess not. What was the bar like?"

"We'll take you. I'll make Jared take us."

Lutie smiled.

"You'll see. The back bar looks as if it were sculptured out of one huge block of chrome. Hanging crystal bar glasses look like a giant chandelier the way the soft lights flicker and reflect through them. The beer is served in chilled burgundy glasses. That's all I had time to see."

"We must go back."

"We shall. Let's see. To enter the dining room you must leave the bar and go through another room where you are greeted by the maitre d'. The dining room is rather dark except for the tables. Each is highlighted by a hanging chrome light. A spotlight. There is a dark-toned carpet which runs from wall to wall and then up the walls to the ceiling. The room dividers are of smoked glass and appear to be mirrors but are not. And on the ceiling there are modern paintings. I know little about modern art. I don't especially like it, living as I do in the midst of cherubs and roses and sunshine. But the whole decorative scheme—the paintings on the ceiling are lighted, by the way—and the darkness, the smoked glass, the glistening crystal and the snowy white linen all help to create a very chic and private-seeming dining room. The sisters' guests were charmed, and poor Charlotte and Adelaide couldn't say one word, except Adelaide did murmur that she had not been there before."

Lutie laughed merrily. "What did you have to eat?"

"We were not offered a menu. Joel had ordered, but I think they don't have a very large selection. You like what they serve or go elsewhere."

"They've always been that way."

"Yes, they have. The thing is, everything is perfectly made and served, the sauces all exquisite. We had a gossamer crêpe—the Crêpe Maison, it was. This was rolled around their crêpe chicken, capped with superb white veloute wine sauce spiced with prosciutto."

"Mmmm-*mmmm*" said Lutie. "Entrée?"

Helen sighed. "Tournedos of beef tenderloin, and calves' liver," she said. "The thinnest possible strips, seasoned with salt, pepper, and flour, fried very quickly in sizzling butter and maybe a dash of white wine added just before being lifted from the fire. Toni always serves the freshest of vegetables in season. We had beautiful green beans cooked with bits of Canadian bacon. And of course, best of all, the dessert, which was a Grand Marnier soufflé—it floated about an inch above the soufflé cup."

"Did the sisters like it?"

"Until they saw the bill. I believe each service came to about thirty dollars."

"Oh, no! Eight people?"

"Eight," said Helen.

"Did Joel pay?"

"Joel had not gone with us. Jared was there in his place, handsome in his dinner coat. He sat and listened to my sisters explain who he was. When they were through, even I didn't know if it was the pope or our houseboy. Anyway, the guests were charmed, and Jared took the bill from Adelaide and paid it.

"Then we went home. I drove one car, Jared drove his, and we took the guests to their hotel and the sisters home. Jared just said softly to me that Joel had been beeped but had not answered. Jared knew where he was, and went to get him."·

"It's hard to remember that he is a doctor. Joel, I mean."

"He is, and a very good one. I thanked Jared, who just chucked me under the chin, and said the soufflé was elegant."

"Which it was."

"Oh, yes."

"What happened afterward?"

"Nothing."

"Didn't the sisters . . .?"

"Try to pay Jared? Maybe they did. He told them, and me, not to talk about the evening."

"To Joel, you mean? But why not? Oh, the case he was called for."

"That's right. He didn't come home until morning, and then only long enough to change. He said he'd get some breakfast at the hospital, and went off again. But Jared later told me what the case was. You know Joel does trauma cases?"

"Yes. I've never really understood . . ."

"They've only recently been made a specialty. They are accidents. Bad, unusual things. Jared doesn't really explain them to me. Last night—all he said was that the worst possible thing that could happen was for a man to rape a baby. A baby three months old."

Lutie stared at her. "But no man would—"

Both women rose from their chairs. Helen put her arm

around the younger woman's shoulders. "Don't speak of it to the boys," she said. "Doctors are human, too, you know."

"I'll bet your sisters—"

"I got to them first. As soon as Jared told me what had happened, I told them not to mention the evening."

"But you told me about it as fun."

"It was fun. And that's the way the men will put it. In their own minds. They couldn't continue to work if they dwelt on the horrors."

Lutie stood very still. "I never understood the doctor business before," she said.

"All doctors are not Jared and Joel, dear."

"I'm going to cry."

"Go right ahead. I did."

"They really are brothers, aren't they?"

"You'd know it when they fight."

"Fight?"

"Argue. Over something important, or whether a tennis ball hit the line. Of course they argue. And I've never heard them mention the dinner at Toni's. The night following, at dinner at our house, they grumbled together about the rise in the cost of scrub suits. Jared told a ridiculous story about some Japanese fellow downtown who dyes them pink and yellow and sells them for golf shirts, or slip-ons at the pool. Jared swore he was going to use his old ones for that, and Joel said, of course, he didn't want somebody to swipe his scrub shirt."

4

At the end of that week, Lutie took Maggie and went to visit her husband's parents. They had invited her. And near-tragedy struck the House.

Largely, the three principals of the home came and went on their own, often telling where and when, but just as often dropping out of sight and knowledge for a day or days at a time. The men checked in at the hospital; Zenobia knew where Miss Helen went and for how long. This was a comfortable arrangement. Information about the absences could crop up as anecdotes. "When I was in Boston last week . . ." Jared might say, or Joel would comment on the different texture of the snow in the California mountains and that of New Hampshire.

Zenobia was told if there were to be guests, but this was largely a matter of groceries and laundry. Adelaide said such arrangements would drive her crazy, Charlotte that she would not put up with it. "You could at least have a bulletin board in the back hall," she suggested. And actually gave them one at Christmas one year. It was never hung.

Helen would leave a note on the desk in her pretty bedroom, with a telephone number. The men could be located through the hospital. What else was needed? Ivory would drive anyone leaving by plane—and gauge the time of their absence by the baggage taken. He would bring the car back and wait for a phone call to be at the airport at a certain time and place. "Dr. Jared he gone to Europe," he would tell his mother. "He went to the foreign office." Perhaps Jared had gone to Europe, perhaps to South America or Australia. If telephone calls came, Zenobia or Ivory would say with honesty, "The doctor is out of town. I dunno when he'll be back."

This system seemed to work. Until the night when Ivory was asked to meet Jared, when he did meet him and brought him back to the House only dimly lighted by the lamp in the hall. Moonlight had turned the outer world to silver. It lay against the House gently, beautifully. Jared told himself that it was good to be home.

"Bring the bags up tomorrow," he told Ivory. "Get back to bed. It's three o'clock."

Ivory knew that. He drove the car around to the garage, and Jared went quietly into the House, bent over to sniff the flowers on the hall table, and softly went up the stairs, looking back over his shoulder at the rooms there. Home. He paused at the door of his mother's room; he'd been gone for two weeks. As softly as he crossed a hospital room, he went into hers, and bent over the bed, straightened quickly and went out.

He went up to his rooms, packed another bag, gathered up a briefcase and some books, and went downstairs again, out to the garage and his car. He drove it to the hospital. His face was like stone.

Joel ran into him at the staff meeting. "I thought you

came home last night," he said. "Did you eat breakfast here?"

"I did," said Jared, his tone icy cold.

"Did you see Helen?"

"Briefly. Please, I'm busy."

Joel watched him stride out of the room. What was eating the guy?

Jared was not at dinner; his car was not in the garage.

The next morning Joel looked at the register. Dr. Jared O'Brien was staying in the medical officer quarters. Joel frowned. As soon as he could, he verified this. Jared did indeed have a suite. He had not been home, and he did not come home for dinner or the weekend.

On Sunday afternoon, Joel hunted him out. "What goes on?" he asked bluntly.

Jared was reading. He looked down again at the page open before him. He sat in a comfortable chair, his feet on a low table. He had dressed his cheek himself.

Joel told this to Helen.

"Didn't you make him say why . . .?"

"Jared isn't the easiest guy to be made to do anything."

"No. But there must be something."

"I'll keep after it. I already found out that he came to the hospital late Sunday night. He sent a wad of clothes to the cleaner. Did anything happen here?"

"At the House? Ivory said he drove him here, then Jared must have taken the car out again. Was he called?"

"I can find that out. I've tried to talk to him. When I went into his rooms again he was on the phone giving someone hell for sending him a patient, reserving the O.R. for a vasectomy, without a complete work-up first."

"That happened today?"

"This afternoon."

"He couldn't have been mad about that on Sunday."

"It's not so much that he's mad, Helen. Something has shocked the guy."

"Should I try to talk to him? I have already phoned and been told that he was busy and not accepting calls." Helen stood up, her face showing her agitation. "I'll go to see him," she declared. "He'll talk to me. I got him to come home from the army hospital. He didn't want to because of his face. But he did. And he continued with his work in the lab he fixed up in one end of the garage. He told us he was developing microsurgical skills so that he could do transplants on humans. Then he worked on kidneys almost entirely."

"Now he does comparatively little kidney work. It's nearly all fertility. Did he go at first to some hospital?"

"Yes. He became a medical resident in a hospital in Michigan, and then one in Australia. When his grandfather developed a bad kidney situation, Brig sent for him and he came home. The staff persuaded him to stay and do research even if he didn't want to work on human patients. That's how he came to be where he is."

"With a beautiful home here—"

"He was very sensitive about his face."

"I can suppose that."

"But the staff doctors did things for him, and when this— he calls it fertility work—when it became so big he worked more and more on that, always developing his manual dexterity."

"He really is wonderful, Helen."

"I know that! And he loves his home here." Joel looked about the handsome room. A fire whispered in the marble hearth. "It has seemed to welcome me," he said softly.

"He has enjoyed you. And you did a great deal for him, physically and mentally."

"So he moves to quarters. I'm going to see the guy, Helen, and make him talk some sense about this."

"Don't fight with him, Joel."

"I shall if that's what it takes."

She reached up to kiss him. "I've enjoyed having you too, dear."

Joel patted her shoulder and shrugged into his topcoat. "I'll come back with my shield or on it," he said drolly.

At the hospital he found Dr. O'Brien giving a lecture to a small group of visiting microbiologists, telling them that a small tremor in a hand need not deter them from attempting to do the things he did with the reversal of a vasectomy. "He knew I was there," Joel told Helen later, "but he went right on talking to the four men."

"Did he let you talk to him before he went on?"

"I followed him and his friends out of the room, and said I had something very important to discuss with him. He took his time about thanking the four doctors for coming, said that he had surgery scheduled for the next day if they would care to stay—I stayed right behind him through the chitchat as he walked them to the front door.

"I followed him up to quarters and into his room. They aren't much, Helen. Comfortable, but bleak. The bedroom is a narrow cell with a bed, a lamp, a small table; the sitting room has an armchair and another chair. A pretty good lamp and table, the doctor's books and a telephone. He has his own bath.

"Jared turned and looked at me. 'Did you come to dress my cheek?' he asked me.

"I said, no, but I would. That he had been doing a very poor job.

"'I thought you would notice that,' said Jared.

"'Can I trust you to stay here while I get my things?'

"'I trust you completely as a doctor,' he said."

Frowning over that statement, Joel did fetch the necessary things and told the desk where he was. "You might phone my home. I think I'll be late for dinner."

He went back to Jared's room and found him stretched out on the bed, reading the newspaper. He only glanced at Joel. "I've never asked you what you used, what you did," he said. "If you'd tell me as you go along—"

Joel did not answer him. He scrubbed his hands, put on gloves and went to work. "Why are you staying here?" he asked as he began.

"Did my mother send you to find out?" Jared asked.

"She is concerned, as I am. As are Zenobia and Ivory."

Jared said nothing.

"We all want to know why you've not come home," said Joel.

"I did come home. Sunday night. Early Monday morning, rather."

"Three A.M., Ivory says."

"That's right. Ordinarily I don't disturb anybody."

"I didn't hear you come in."

"Damned right you didn't!" snapped Jared.

"Don't talk or move for a few minutes," said the doctor, working over the scarred cheek. Jared's eyes studied the face. Joel was well aware of that. But he worked steadily, his hands firm. "I guess it is hard—to do it—on one's own cheek," he said, getting ready to apply the dressing and the mask. He studied the latter. "Haven't you a fresh one?"

"At home I have a box of them. You can fetch them here."

"You don't mean to come home with me?"

"I do not."

75

Joel gathered the debris of his surgery and wrapped it in a paper towel. Then he sat down in the chair. "Why not?" he asked.

"You'll be late for dinner."

"I phoned. Why aren't you coming home?"

"I think you know. Sunday night I went into Helen's room. I wanted to kiss her cheek. And—in bed with her— you *know* what I found!"

"Brig," said Joel quietly. "Helen has a right to life. I wish she'd marry the man. He—"

"The man I found was *you!*" said Jared loudly. "Now I understand all about the rights of life. I execute them myself at times. But incest— That I cannot and won't take, Joel! And you can tell Helen so!"

"I just stared at him," Joel told Jared's mother.

She had gone stone white. "Even if it were true . . . ," she whispered.

"It hit me like a shot," said Joel, continuing his tale, speaking with difficulty. "He just lay there on the bed, looking at the ceiling. And he said something ridiculous about sex being an integral part of the human soma—

"'And incest as well?' I asked him.

"He flared then. He jumped to his feet, and he swore and said something about whatever I believed or wanted to believe. And I asked him if he meant to return home. Or was he trying to get rid of me? That could easily have been done before all this turned up. I said I was only dimly aware of what in hell he meant by soma, but incest there was not nor could have been.

"And *he* said he had almost pulled me out of your bed and given me the beating of my life. I replied that it would be an 'almost' for any reason. I did not want to fight him, then for your sake, now for the hospital's. But if he was so inclined, I'd go for him right then. And see what he could do.

"Oh, I talked, and talked, and finally I told him that the person he must talk to was you. But that certainly I would leave the house. And at once."

"Joel, you won't."

"I'll have to, Helen. He may ask me to come back. But so long as he thinks . . ."

"He isn't thinking. He was shocked. He is feeling that shock with jealousy. It is his home. But I'll marry Brig before I'll let this split up our family."

"Let me talk to Brig."

"Well, if you want to. Oh, the whole thing shocks me. I never thought Jared—" She got up and left the room, but returned after an hour.

"Tell me," she said. "I—I— Didn't he think I should . . ."

"He was shocked at the idea that it was I there with you. And when I could think about it, I would have been just as shocked."

"Yes. Yes, of course."

"But it was his mistaken idea of incest," said Joel. "That's what hit him Sunday night."

"And you *have* come to be a son to me. I'll agree. But I wouldn't dream of doing— Brig comes occasionally. We'd have a date, and—he'd stay. I wish I had married him."

"You're not to do it, now. Just because of this."

"Didn't Jared know—or guess?" Helen asked. "I thought that was why he moved up to the attic."

"It could have been the reason."

Helen sat, head down, a picture of sorrow.

"But, that night, he was sure it was I. There was light enough—"

"There could not have been."

"Does Brig know?"

"I asked Jared that, and he said that you would tell him, and he'd speak to Brig. He will have to believe him. And me. But he just sat and stared at me. It was the filthy idea of incest, he kept saying."

"And there was no incest."

"I talked about that to him, I drew diagrams. There is no blood relationship between you and me, Helen. And finally he agreed. He says he'll come and apologize."

"To me? And stay here?"

"He made no promises."

It was a sorry time, what Joel called a sticky time. Jared did return home, and Brig came to the house, but only when one of the boys was also there. They all missed him. And were relieved when he took off on one of his trips. "I can't think what there is in Hawaii for him to see," said Jared.

When Jared had returned home, it was as if he never had been anywhere but on one of his lecture trips. Helen kissed him and said it was good to have him back. "I find I need two sons," she said at dinner.

But it was not the same. Joel went back to the attic room that he had first occupied. Brig seldom came except for an hour or so. He went to Hawaii and then on a long tour of South America.

The doctors gave Helen what she called orders. If she had places she wanted to go at night, she was to tell them. They would arrange for one of them to be her escort.

"I shouldn't like that," she told them. "I have no wish to be a duty or burden on either of you."

"But we enjoy the theater, the galas at the opera house," Joel told her.

"You maybe. Not Jared."

"Well, he's the weird one."

Jared flushed, and Joel apologized. "I know I am called weird at the hospital," said Jared. "Who isn't?"

"Not quite in the same way. I talk to people. I attend hospital parties."

"I understand you can dance a jig," drawled Jared.

Joel laughed. "I don't do the steps right. Just throw my feet around. The girls like it."

"The girls," murmured Helen.

"They are always pairing Joel off with somebody," said Jared.

"Don't you have a secretary?" Helen asked.

"I do. A man."

"Oh, dear," sighed his mother. "What about your head operating room nurse?"

"She's ten years older than I am, and has a mustache."

They all laughed at this.

"And the patients he has," offered Joel, "are no help."

"Why not?" Helen began to ask, then she flushed. "No, I guess they wouldn't be."

Jared stood up, to his full height, which was tall. "I wish you two would quit planning my life," he said. "I'll be bringing some girl home and telling you that I'll marry her, and you'll both go into a dither."

"Try us," Joel suggested.

But he did not. Not right away. He and Joel had words one evening about a committee Jared had let himself go on.

It was a stormy evening, and on the hearth the fire was welcome.

"You can't do it, and keep up your schedule of surgery," Joel assured him. "They'll send you around to talk to school boards and senior high-school students."

"I hope so," said Jared quietly.

Helen's head lifted. "What's going on?" she asked.

Jared looked at Joel, and nodded. "You explain to her," he said. "You feel more strongly about it than I do."

Helen dropped her knitting. "Joel?" she prompted.

"Well, the guy's dead right," he admitted, speaking slowly. "But can you play the piano and mix biscuits at the same time?"

Even Jared laughed.

"I've never tried," Helen confessed. "But now you must tell me."

"Oh," Joel began, his eyes on Jared, who had tipped back in his chair and closed his eyes, "you know how the guy is always writing books and articles?"

"He does it very well, too."

"That's secondary."

Jared's eyes popped open. "Try it sometime," he suggested.

"Not me. I know a cushy job when I have one."

Jared snorted. Then he turned to his mother. "There's a theory," he said, "that a microsurgeon has to work every day, and he must never, never, never take a week off without operating."

"But—"

"We know different, don't we? Now, there's another thing you know. I've talked about it."

"Oh, lawdy, has he talked about it?" Joel groaned.

Jared tried not to laugh. "Anyway, I *am* serious about it. And I have mentioned it. And when the Medical Association formed a committee to examine the status of premedical education, I spoke up."

"And not in his sleep, either," said Joel. "So, of course he's on the committee to examine, and perhaps—that will

80

become *probably*—change the premedical requirements for a guy wanting to get into medical school."

"Well, it seems ridiculous to me," said Jared, "for a chap to go through high school and premed, studying enough German to make use of a text, know the nouns and verbs mainly—he puts in a semester at this futility. He studies a little botany, of all things, a little chemistry—and presents himself as a candidate for a course in the reality of medical school, where he studies the same things, but deeply, intently, and carefully. Usefully. But if you ask him to write a theme, or even a paragraph in a blue book, the chap can't do it. His handwriting is atrocious; he can't compose a sentence, let alone a paragraph. And could he make a speech before a class or a group of medics at a convocation? No, he could not. So I say, leave the dissected frog, the wafer-thin slices of a mushroom, the painful, and poor, drawings of the eye's structure out of premed. And study H. L. Mencken or William Shakespeare, or a course in daily theme writing. Your med school professor isn't going to know whether a student has had premed zoology or not. He approaches each freshie confident that he doesn't know a damn thing, and he takes his hot little hand and leads him through the structure of the eye, the brain, and the complications of the knee." He paused for breath and watched Helen and Joel wipe the tears of laughter from their eyes.

"I'm serious," he said. "We'll get better graduating doctors my way."

"But you can't do your work at the hospital, and go around to colleges and medical schools—"

"I don't plan to do it. My work, as you call it. I have doctors at the hospital who can do my vasectomies—or their own, which will be just as good. And I'll come back after my work with this committee. For one thing, they do

81

not ask me to do a thing but instruct speakers to carry my message."

"Fat chance," said Joel.

"If you aren't really needed," Helen said doubtfully.

Jared smiled at her gently. "I think I need a change of scene," he said. "Joel keeps telling me I don't know people, and I don't. I don't believe it would work if I tried preaching to the people who have known me professionally, or in the church. I think the places the committee will send me to will afford me the chances I need—or I hope they will."

"We'll miss you," said Joel.

"I may chicken out. That option is open to me, but I am serious about meeting the new people. I think it is more than time I considered starting my own family, and I can't see any prospect of success in that venture here."

"Don't say that sort of thing to the nurses, hen-medics, or even the choir members of your church," said Joel.

"There's Lutie," Helen murmured.

Jared made no answer to that.

Joel stood up and stretched his arms. "I'd better get to bed," he said. "I didn't sleep very well last night."

"You kept running up and down the stairs," Jared agreed. "I've meant to ask you why."

"I was checking to see if I had turned off the oven."

Both Helen and Jared gaped at him.

"Shut your mouths," Joel said, laughing. "You'll catch a fly. I'll explain. Remember? Last night I got beeped half-way through dinner."

"I remember what you said," drawled Jared.

"I'll apologize to Helen, but I've heard you say worse."

"Tell your story."

"Yes, Big Brother, I mean to. I got beeped. I didn't finish my dinner. I came home at one-thirty, hungry as a bear. The night service at this boardinghouse is terrible. I went into the kitchen and made myself a toasted cheese sandwich."

"Did you clear away?" asked Helen. "Zenobia—"

"I'm afraid of her too," said Joel. "Yes, I cleared way. Ate the sandwich—you're low on sharp cheddar—and I went up to bed. For a while I didn't sleep . . ."

"Too much cheese," said Jared.

"There wasn't that much cheese," Joel retorted. "But I lay there; I went over my day, which is a bad habit I have, and I came up to that sandwich and I began to wonder if I had turned off the oven—so I finally got up and went down to look."

"It was off," said Helen.

"It was, but the oven was warm to my touch. I wondered if something was wrong and the thing wouldn't turn off."

"They stay warm for a time."

"Well, this one did. But the red light was off, and I went upstairs again—"

"And stumbled over the last step," said Jared.

"Gee, you did stay awake."

"Why not? You made things sound as if the house was coming down. I almost got up and gave you a sleeping pill."

"I went to sleep. And do you know what? I kept dreaming of that red oven light. And what Zenobia would say to me in the morning."

"So you overslept, and she said them to me," Jared told him. "You can't fool Zenobia."

"She is fussy about her stove," murmured Helen.

"She'd be fussier if I got a small oven up in my room."

"Oh, yes, she would!" Helen agreed. "She's quite sure one of you is going to burn the house down."

"Or break a leg on the top step," said Jared, standing up. "I have to go, Mum. I'll look at the oven light as I go out."

Joel lifted his coffee cup and drank from it. "D'you think he meant what he said about getting married?" he asked.

"If he has Lutie in mind, yes," said Helen.

"And I don't think he'll give a year to this premed education thing either," said Joel.

"It's important."

"So is the work he does."

"He knows that. I think I'll marry Brig while he's gone."

Joel looked up, surprised. "Why?"

"You boys have gone around me like wary cats ever since that night—"

"Well, we had a different picture of you, sweetheart."

"These are modern days."

"But you don't have a modern son. And I—Well, do what you want. We like Brig."

"But you'll be jealous of him."

"That's a fact. Up to now, you've been our girl. To look out for, to protect. But it's your life."

"And Jared thinks he can point that out by having a wife of his own."

"He'd point it out, that's a fact. But I'm like you. Unless it's Lutie . . . "

"Do you think he'll go?"

"Not for a year. He'll be making trips to talk to college boards and such. He does feel strongly about this premed thing. And we'll miss him at the center. But he's not going to be away for long stretches."

"He's never done it before. Once he did something in Switzerland for three months. I finally joined him."

Joel laughed. "Mother hen."

Helen nodded. "I've been lucky. He's let me be one. And speaking of bachelors, there's you."

"Oh—" Joel got up from his chair.

"Jared says you're a charmer."

"So is he. Only, he can't forget his face."

"Could you?"

"Maybe not. And I agree that Jared has a right to live his life as he wants to live it."

"Did you know that he thinks he interferes with your life?"

Joel had reached the door. He came back. "How's that?"

"By making you live in the attic with him, and other obligations."

"Zenobia and you."

"Being a man alone, rather."

Joel stood silent for a second. "Well, I'll be goldarned," he said then, softly. "I think I'll go up and pack his bag. A year, did he say?"

"He'll be on the board for a year."

"Then that's how long his mind will be on other things."

He went out, shaking his head.

Jared was appointed to the committee. He went to the West Coast and spoke to five universities. He called home about three times a week and was told that he was missed. At home, and at the hospital, the medical school.

Before Thanksgiving he said he was returning for three days, he needed some heavier clothes, and he was bringing a girl home with him. Would Joel please stay on the third floor?

"I'll get out completely," Joel offered.

"That won't be necessary. And don't tell the med school."

"The boss will know."

"I suppose. Has there been much talk?"

"All coming to the same conclusion. That you're as queer as a blue watermelon."

Jared laughed. "She's a pretty girl."

"Good! I'll get a haircut."

5

Joel did talk at the hospital. He said that Jared had gone off to find a girl he could marry and so have a family.

He told this at a staff lunch table and his listeners stared at him, unbelieving. "We have girls here," said one man.

"I don't think the guy ever saw them."

The men sat speechless. "He's smart in other ways."

"Yes, he is. But he does things his way."

"She'd be a lucky girl."

"If he loves her, yes."

That question hung in Joel's mind. It was there when Jared and "the girl" arrived.

He went out to the car to greet them. The girl had gotten out of the car and stood looking up at the House.

"It looks like a farmhouse," she told the second doctor.

"We like it."

She accepted Jared's arm and went up the steps, Joel following closely behind. "With his mouth open a foot wide," Zenobia told Helen, who waited in the living room.

The girl was a tall one, slender. She was wearing a pair of brown tailored slacks, a print blouse in a lighter brown with some red in it. Her dark hair was brushed smoothly against her head.

"She looks like a model," Helen told herself.

They came into the house, Joel carrying two bags. His face wooden, his eyes watchful. The girl—her name was Jeanne, Jeanne MacDonald. She looked wide-eyed about the hall, brushed her fingertips across the flowers on the table.

Jared touched her elbow and she went into the formal parlor. Sun streamed in through the wide bay window and brightened the colors of the carpet and the richly upholstered chairs. She tilted her head back and looked up.

Her hand clapped across her mouth. "Oh, no!" she said clearly enough. "Not *cherubs!*" She glanced at Jared. "Not really?" she asked.

"You really live here?" she went on, freeing herself from his hand and walking around the lovely room, looking up at the painted ceiling, the elaborate border that was more than a molding. She stumbled over a velvet chair, impatiently pushed it aside and came to the fireplace, the beveled mirror, laid her head against the mantel, and laughed.

Joel looked at Helen, and they both looked at Jared.

"I'll take your bags up to your rooms," he said clearly.

"Do they have cupids, too?" asked Jeanne, still laughing. Jared did not answer.

"It's an old house," said Helen quietly, but, oh, so firmly. "And we love it."

"I'm sorry," said the girl. "But—" She went over to Jared. "You really *like* it?" she asked him.

"He does," Joel answered for him. "And down the hill there is a nice river with little stones along the edge. You can do a Virginia Woolf any time you want to."

Jeanne looked puzzled. "Who's Virginia Woolf?" she asked.

Helen touched her arm. "Come with me, dear," she said softly. "You'll want to rest and clean up a bit before dinner. My sisters, Jared's aunts, are coming this evening."

Jared stared at her. "They aren't, really?" he asked.

"Yes. Of course they would want to meet the girl you were bringing home."

"I'll take the bags," Joel offered. "You can explain to Miss MacDonald what strange people the O'Briens are."

"I'll let Jared do that when he takes her for a walk after dinner," said Helen, her tone more acid than the men had ever heard it.

She followed Joel up the stairs. Behind them Jared was explaining to Jeanne how and when the House had been built.

"Seduce her if you can," Helen told Joel. "You don't think Jared has committed himself?"

"I'll have his beeper activated," Joel promised. "And I'll drive Miss Woolf to the plane myself tomorrow."

They got through the evening. They let the aunties do their best, or worse, to entertain Jared's young lady.

"Do you have any idea of how busy Jared can be?" Aunt Adelaide asked her. "Or are you in the medical field yourself?"

"Miss MacDonald is a curator of a university library," said Jared stiffly.

"She's very pretty," murmured Aunt Charlotte. "Is she here long enough to come for dinner at our house?"

Joel looked up at the twinkling lights of the coffered ceiling. Pot roast, carrots and potatoes, a tomato and lettuce salad, lemon pie— He touched his napkin to his lips. "I don't think so," he answered.

And just then Jared's beeper went off. Startled, he looked at Joel, who nodded. "There's a waiting line," he said blandly. "I told them you'd be in tonight."

"I'll talk to you later," said Jared stiffly.

"I'll be available. And I'll take care of Miss Woolf," he added.

Jared looked appealingly at his mother. "She's a guest in our home," he said stiffly.

"Joel," said Helen, "don't you think you should drive Jared to the hospital?"

"We left quite a hen party behind," Joel said when Jared joined him in the car.

"You couldn't have arranged it," said Jared.

"I swear I did nothing but say that you would be home this evening, and that activated your beeper."

They did not speak again until they reached the parking garage. "I thought you all wanted me to marry and raise a family," said Jared.

"Couldn't you find someone who liked cupids?" drawled Joel.

"I thought any girl— I tell you I am not the type. Let me alone, will you?"

"Yes, Doctor," said Joel. "Yes, sir! We certainly will. But tell me, if she's a librarian, why doesn't she know who Virginia is, or was?"

"*Virginia* does not inhabit the shelves of a medical library," said Jared. "What do I have here?"

"A child injured his hand, nearly cut off a finger."

"Good. I mean, maybe work is what I need."

"We'll take care of Miss MacDonald until she leaves."

"I can attend to that," Jared promised him. "Are you coming up with me?"

"Of course. I've been keeping things bright and shining for you."

They went up the stairs to the main floor, Jared's hand warmly on Joel's shoulder. "Do you want to scrub?" he asked when they went across to surgical.

"It's a joy to watch you in your own field," said his brother.

It was a joy. To see Jared's sure skill with the small child and the miniscule instruments. "A guy can't let a boy grow up without all his fingers," Joel commented to the scrub nurse. "Remind me to ask Jared if he has any plans to marry that girl he brought home tonight."

The nurse's head jerked. "Has he . . .?" she gasped. "Did he . . . ?"

Joel shrugged.

The women in the hospital had long had their eyes on Jared O'Brien.

"What about you?" growled Jared, shrugging off his mask, dropping it and his gown into the can, or reasonably close to it. He went out to the desk, and asked for his microsurgical charts. He sat and read every one of them. Joel lounged in a chair and dozed.

"I'll look at the child," said Jared, rising, somewhat stiffly.

"And then I think it will be safe to go home," Joel agreed.

They did those things, going quietly across to the house, inside, and very quietly up the stairs to the third floor.

"You folks have deviled me about marrying and having a family," said Jared, when he came out of the shower.

"But not one of us considered the chance that she, or they, would look like Aunt Charlotte," said Joel.

Jared stared at him, and they laughed, laughed hard, laughed loud.

"Get some sleep, will you?" Jared said, sliding between the sheets. "But you'd better get it up here."

Joel nodded and went to his bedroom.

"Helen told me to seduce her," he called back to Jared.

"I'll speak to my mother on that subject," said Jared. "Go to sleep."

Miss MacDonald departed the next day, saying that she had remembered an obligation she had forgotten about.

Jared took her to the plane, and went on to the hospital. He would have to fill the engagements he had made to speak for the educational matter, but the hospital would set up appointments for him. He was ready to go to work, and there was work aplenty. The little fellow whose finger he had returned to his hand was doing fine.

"You should have kids of your own, Doctor," the mother told him gratefully.

"I'd like nothing better," said Jared.

"He's a great man," the mother told the nurse.

"Too smart, or too great, to live like the rest of us," said the woman in white.

Jared finished his project and was at home again. But there was a change in him. Joel mentioned this to Helen.

"He never believed us when we told him you were not the man in bed with me that night."

"Good Lord! What do we do?"

"Silence my sisters some way."

Joel frowned at her. "How did they get into the act?"

"They are in every act of my life. They have made fools of themselves about your staying here while Jared's been away on these trips."

"I make a helluva chaperone."

"Do I have to marry Brig to persuade them?"

"No. But I'll move out."

92

Helen rose and came to him where he lounged deep in a chair. "I love you like a son, Joel," she told him. "Jared knows my feeling—"

"Something's eating the guy. I've thought of sending for Lutie."

"I wish she'd come. But we can't send for her."

Helen stood gazing out across the lawn to the river. "When he was a little boy," she said, "he would gather a sand pail full of pebbles down near the river and he would outline the shadows on the lawn with the little rocks. Of course the shadows would move, and his work didn't mean anything. He tried to find someone who had moved the stones. It took a time to explain to him about sun's moving."

"Or the earth's."

"Yes. But he put in a couple of years trying to see if the time would come when the sun and shadow would exactly meet again."

"And they never did again."

"That's right. He remembers what things were like with Lutie and him before he went to Vietnam. They were very young, you know. And the injury to his face must have been something like the time your father told me he was going to divorce me."

"Tell us about that," said Jared from the doorway.

Joel straightened in his chair. "Don't you know?" he asked.

"Do you?"

"Not me. The bishop never got that close to me."

"The bish . . ." Jared began, then he nodded. "Sometimes I forget who you are," he confessed, coming out to sit on the steps. He kicked off his shoes. "I've had a stand-up day," he apologized.

"Yes. Well—"

"My grandmother here told me one version," said Jared. "Aunt Charlotte told me one when I was ten."

"Charlotte?" cried Helen.

"Of course. She knows everything and gets everything wrong. I knew that you and I lived here instead of at their house in the city, and that suited me fine. But no one ever really told me why."

Helen drew a deep breath. "You were just a baby," she said.

"And we lived in his parents' home," Jared agreed. "This house, which I love."

"That's right."

"And Lutie lived next door."

Helen and Joel laughed. "A half-mile next door," said Helen.

"Close enough. I didn't need any brothers or sisters. Lutie and I—"

"We know that story," growled Joel. "So let Helen tell hers. Then I can finish it. I knew the bishop better than anyone."

"Charlotte—my sisters—" said Helen slowly, "have always blamed me. Because he was a clergyman."

"When they're rats," said Joel calmly, "they're big rats."

"But I didn't know that. What puzzles me now is that I seem not to have discussed this with Jared."

"You didn't," said her son. "I thought it was because of the disgrace. A disgrace, incidentally, which I have always carried in my mind."

"But you went to church with me. You still work in the church."

"I couldn't blame the church. I knew there had to be a shame, a secret disgrace. Joel's appearance has forced the

94

issue to be repeated in my thoughts. I've planned, a dozen times, to ask you, or someone. I knew what Granny told me, and Aunt Charlotte, were fairy tales. I looked it up in the newspaper files, so I knew it was not a crime or that sort of disgrace." He sat staring out at the river, shining in the late sunlight. "So—tell me."

"I know what happened," said Joel.

"And you don't want to talk about it."

"I don't *want* to, but I shall. First, excuse me for a minute." Abruptly, he left their little group, walked into the house.

"He does that at the hospital," said Jared. "When there is a decision to be made, or he is asked to make a report on something. He'll ask to be excused for a minute, and he leaves abruptly. He never explains—"

"He's a nice boy, Jared."

"I like him. I feel a real brother to him."

Helen sighed. "I hoped you would." She slapped at a mosquito.

"Let's sit inside the porch," said Jared, rising to give her a hand.

Joel joined them quietly. He sat close to Helen and held her hand. "Tell me what you knew of the bishop," he said quietly.

"He wasn't a bishop when I knew him," she said readily. "He was the curate, then a priest of the church that I attended. All the women were crazy about him. Choir, altar workers—married, unmarried. He was young and handsome, looked like Jared."

"But no hole in his cheek," said Jared quietly.

"No. He had nothing wrong that I could see." She paused and sat looking out at the lawn, the river. "My sisters—" she began, and stopped. "When he began to come to see me, when he asked for a date, my mother and my sisters opposed my accepting his interest. I couldn't, myself, believe it was real. I was popular with boys of my own age, but I had never gone out with anyone his age—he was twenty-four— When he asked my parents if he could marry me, I was as surprised as they were. I think they agreed, thinking I would then be safe. Because I was popular, I suspect they worried about me. Anyway, they said yes, if I wanted things that way."

"And you did."

Helen's face flushed, her eyes shone. "Of course I did. I thought I was the luckiest girl in the world, and within three months we had a wedding. And came here to his parents' home for a honeymoon. I was shocked when his mother cried when she saw me. She turned to my new husband accusingly and said, 'You married a child!'

"His father hushed her and embraced me. I always loved him."

"So did I," said Jared somberly. "What was the problem?"

"Well, it seems there had been a scandal in which my husband—before he was my husband—was involved. A man was almost killed. They had had a fight in the church. I never wanted to know the details, but— Well, Joel evidently knows the whole thing. It seems that your father was blamed though he was not charged and arrested. However, he took the blame. His mother told me he had been framed. They were glad when the church accepted his side of the story, glad that he took a church many miles away, on the far side of the diocese. They were glad to know that he was going to be married. They felt as he did that the truth would defend him, but that I would be too young to

96

face the gossip and the charges. They were right, of course. But I became pregnant at once, and had my lovely blond-haired baby, and I heard nothing that I didn't want to hear.

"During your second year I came to spend Christmas here with his parents, and he brought me, though Christmas is such a busy time for a clergyman. By then he had a new church, remember. But he brought me here and at Christmas dinner he told me that he wanted a divorce. I could get it. If not, he would. Your grandparents were horrified and told me to stay with them. His father got in touch with the bishop. I was in shock, and I didn't know, and don't remember, the details. I had this house to shelter me, and help in caring for you, and I signed some papers." She sat silent, smoothing a handkerchief she held against the chair arm, looking at it.

"He got his divorce all right," said Joel roughly. "And immediately married the wife of the man he had almost killed. She had been working at the church as secretary."

Helen nodded. "I knew that. My mother and sisters went away for a while, to avoid all the talk, they said."

"Did he attack that man?" Jared asked. "Why?"

"They had a fight. Over the bishop's attentions to my mother. The bishop reached for something—it happened to be a heavy brass lamp. And he struck the fellow just right. It could have killed him."

"He wasn't a bishop then."

"No, of course not. But he was a clergyman. And there was a scandal. Our father took the line that he was not to blame, that the truth would defend him. But his bishop suspended him, and he had to find a job. Which he did. He sold insurance and was very good at it. My mother told me when I was ready to go to med school that she had not

97

wanted him to divorce you, Helen. She said you could have saved his reputation and he might have stayed in the church."

Helen looked shocked. "I didn't know what was going on. I didn't know he was having an affair."

"Did you know he'd fought this guy?"

"I knew there had been a fight. In the church. I was getting ready to come up here—moving the baby. I was just dumb. Perhaps I could have kept him doing his work for the church."

"And he wouldn't have had to marry my mother, or bring little me into this world . . .," drawled Joel.

"What was he like?" asked Jared. "To my knowledge, I never saw him."

"Oh, he was a go-getter. And after a time a new presiding bishop let him become a priest again. He built up churches as he had built up his insurance business. And eventually he himself became a bishop. The ladies adored him."

"Yes," said Helen sadly. "We did. What about you, Joel?"

"Well—there were things . . . for one, he always slept until noon, and didn't want a sound in the house. My mother stayed with him. I had a nursemaid until I was four, then I learned to get up and find a breakfast for myself. I was here by accident, I suppose. They could not have wanted a child. I did yard work. Things. He agreed to pay my tuition to school, and I went away when I was fourteen. To prep, college, and med. I spent my vacations on my own. I even came here one time and looked the city and the family over. I went to Nam immediately after med. And the bishop got himself killed in a sailing accident. The newspaper story was that he'd gone out alone to meditate and a storm came up. But don't ever believe any story you may hear about him."

"He did send you to school, Joel," said Helen.

"I blackmailed him."

She opened her lips to protest, then shook her head. "Yes," she said.

"I didn't think much about Jared here until he began to get his name in the journals about his microsurgery. I wanted to know him. But I just asked for a job at the hospital center. They needed me. It took six months for Jared to discover I was there."

Jared sat, thoughtful. "I'm not sure I believe all this," he said, as if speaking to himself. Speaking his thoughts aloud. "I don't see how all this could happen."

Joel said nothing. He had told his story, and the shock of it showed in his face, his eyes.

"I don't either," said Helen. "Now I don't. Then—I was young. I had been dreadfully hurt. Numb with that hurt. My ideal romance—my idea of a priest of the church— There was nowhere I could turn to find relief or a way out. Others took over for me. Your grandparents, Jared, this house sheltered me. I had only a few friends here. I had you to cuddle and care for."

"And Aunt Charlotte and Aunt Adelaide . . . ," said Jared gruffly.

Helen reached out to touch his hand. "They talked about the disgrace and how embarrassing it was for them."

"It wasn't *their* disgrace!" cried Joel. "And I don't see that it was in any way yours."

"My marriage had failed. I must have done something . . . "

"Oh, you did not. I wasn't around but I knew the man in question."

"How did you come through?" Jared asked Helen, a doctor's curiosity in his voice. "You must have been depressed."

"I suppose I was. But it was your grandfather who pulled me through. We worked on the grounds together. He encouraged me to do volunteer work. And he always made a place for you in his life."

"I'll bet the aunts said it was his money."

"They did. And I was grateful that he had it. But I think if he had not been a rich man he still would have given me strength, and a place to live."

"Grandma . . . "

"Yes, we both loved her. She made the House our home. It was through her that you loved this house, and the cupids, the big rooms. She blamed herself for having spoiled her son. I don't to this day know how she had such a son, except that he and she had the same charming ways. She was a darling. He used his charms . . . "

She fell silent, and the men waited on her.

"She didn't spoil me," said Jared finally. "I think she might have, but Grandpa wouldn't let her. I remember times when I wanted something—a bicycle—and he said I had to earn the money to pay for it. She went and bought me one, and he took it back to the store."

"He rode it," said Helen. "Grandma said he looked ridiculous."

"Did he?"

"Yes, I think he did. You and I stood on the porch here, Jared, and watched him. I remember that, don't you?"

"I remember the row I raised."

They all laughed at the pictured scene.

"Did you ever get the bike?" Joel asked.

"I had one, so I guess I earned it. I don't remember how."

"I do," said Helen. "You did jobs like cleaning the stable where Lutie's pony was kept."

"Gee whiz!" said Jared. "I remember *that!*"

"It was the smell of your character building," Joel assured him.

"It made me glad to go away to military school."

"Did you do that?" Joel asked. "I'll bet you looked just darling in your uniform."

Jared kicked him. Hard.

Helen was shocked.

They often talked this way, about a dozen things. This was the first time Joel had brought the past so vividly before them. Jared could see that young boy filling in the morning hours until his parents chose to rise, scrabbling his own breakfast, going to school . . .

The pictures kept rising before him. Through that same father, his own life had been incredibly pleasant, the beautiful home, Zenobia, his sweet grandmother, strong grandfather, and Helen. He thought about it during the night, and again the next day he found that the pictures which he had conjured were interfering with his work. He had patient interviews scheduled, and he found himself wanting to ask the patient why he wished to be sterilized, what his wife was like—things over and beyond his privilege as a doctor. Those who wanted correction brought even more questions to his mind. This had never before happened to him. A patient was that and no more. He owed and gave his interest, but to question his home life, his family situation—that was beyond his privilege. He didn't *want* personal knowledge of his patients. Could he believe their replies to his question? What difference should it make to him?

He surely had discipline enough . . .

He began to want to know the patient's immediate background. What sort of home did he have? Could he meet the wife? She might be opposed to this move. Should the doctor question her? Was the man doing this drastic thing because of her? With her consent and knowledge? Without it?

He had sometimes asked a question or two, but he had never before wanted to enter their lives, see their houses, their homes. Was there a Helen in the background? A small, bright-eyed Joel raking leaves from under a hedge?

Finally he gave up. It was the first time such panic, so many doubts, had descended upon him. He cancelled two appointments, and told his office secretary that he was going home.

"Are you sick, Dr. O'Brien?"

Maybe Tucker could tell him? Jared did not know. "Do you think Dr. Klopman can fit them in?"

"If you are ill, he can."

Jared reached for his suit jacket. "I can't finish the list," he said shortly. "If Klopman doesn't want to, maybe the patient will return at another time. I am going home."

"Yes, Doctor." Tucker made a note on his desk pad, and looked with concern after his boss. Dr. O'Brien had never before done such a thing. Rather, he worked too hard, took on too much.

Jared knew that as well as Tucker did. He was frightened. If his profession should fail him . . .

He could talk to one of the shrinks, he could talk to Joel,

to his mother. He could talk to himself, take a long walk and get his mind in order again.

That early morning—he had wanted to talk to the man's wife, his family. Being a good microsurgeon was not all there was to life. Now there were things to do. He must look at the patient for whom, at Joel's request, he had worked skillfully and successfully that morning. Was he doing all right? He was still in intensive care. "To keep him from talking," said the nurse. The patient was apparently asleep.

He checked at the desk and signed out. The nurses knew he had other patients. He made no effort to explain. They watched him go down the long corridor, tall, slender, erect, his shoulders as square as a box, the light gleaming on his blond hair.

Not for the first time they asked why Dr. O'Brien had never married. "Too many dames are willing," said the intern at the desk behind them. For a minute the nurses were silenced, then they laughed. Yes, that could be the reason.

"Dr. Joel O'Brien is cute, too," said the aide.

Yes, he was.

"He has more fun being single," said the intern.

"You're too smart," the floor nurse told him.

While all this was going on, Jared was making his way downstairs, through the halls, across the garage. The attendant was surprised to see him. "You got through early," he told the doctor, giving him his keys.

"I'm playing hookey," Jared said seriously.

And he was. He felt guilty about doing so, too. Why didn't he turn on his heel and go back to finish the work he was paid to do?

But the way he had felt since midmorning. . . . He was almost disappointed to find Helen struggling against a stiff breeze to fasten the pyrocanthus vine more securely to the corner of the garage. The wind kept blowing her scarf across her face. Jared rescued her, and tied the vine.

"What are you doing home?" his mother asked him.

"I came to tie up your vine."

"Mhmmmmn. Let's go inside. My mouth is full of hair."

They went in through the kitchen and Jared had to tell Zenobia why he was home so early.

"What if I said I'd got fired?" he asked her.

"It ain't like you to fib to me," said the big woman, "but I long ago learned when you was doin' it."

Jared laughed, and followed his mother down the hall, hung her sweater and scarf on a hook in the closet, and asked her if they might light a fire.

"It's your house, darling," she said. "Neither Zenobia nor I should ask why you came home early."

"But you both did it."

He went up the stairs three at a time. Helen tidied her hair and waited for him to come down. He had changed to corduroy slacks and a pull-on shirt. He knelt before the fireplace in the back sitting room. The wind whistled around the corner of the house.

He waited until the fire caught, then took up the morning paper and sat down in the corner of the couch. His mother was knitting. She kept glancing at her son. Finally she spoke as he had known she would. "What's wrong, Jared?" she asked quietly.

"Nothing."

Her hands dropped to her lap, her head went up. "Now, Jared—"

He nodded. "I couldn't concentrate," he said. "And I can't work if my mind goes floating off to other things."

She nodded, in her turn. "It's the same with knitting," she said.

This made him laugh, and again she nodded. "Didn't you work, today?"

"Of course I worked. I even did a job for Joel this morning."

"Can't Joel do his own work?"

"He can and does. But he gets accidents with complications. He had one this morning. I don't know if I should tell a lady about it."

"I'm not a 'lady.'"

"No. Not in this sense. Well—he had a man who fell into a rotary saw and it caught—cut—right across his—excuse me, Mrs. O'Brien—across his penis. Cut it off as neat as you cut that thread."

She gasped. "You couldn't sew it back on."

"I couldn't but I did."

"Oh, Jared." Her voice, her eyes, adored this son of hers.

"I don't know if I was *wonderful,* or not. Joel thought I might be. I've never done this sort of job before. It's been done. They brought the man and what Zenobia used to call his petooter straight to the hospital trauma bay. Joel told me to try."

"He helped?"

"Lord, yes. A dozen people helped. He packed the thing in ice, put the fellow under sedation, and we worked. Took until noon."

"Did you eat lunch?"

"I think so. I had patients scheduled. A class that was cancelled."

"Do you think . . . ?"

"I did the best vessel and nerve work I knew how. But we won't know until days. The poor guy—young—I know of only three jobs like this successfully done. Not here. I've never seen it done. Just read about it."

"It will work. Is doubt what brought you home early?"

"No. I often have doubts and handle them. Today—lately, Helen—" He broke off. "When did I start calling you 'Helen'?"

"When you came back from Vietnam. Mother and my sisters disapproved, so you kept it up."

Jared laughed. "We let them decide a lot of things for us, don't we?"

She was startled. "Ye—es," she agreed. "I think we do."

"I'll call you what I like. In front of them, anyway."

"No, no! In front of yourself, Jared," she said firmly.

He nodded and said no more. She watched him furtively. After a half hour, she spoke. "Don't you want to call and ask Joel how his patient is?" she asked.

"He'd ask me why I came home, leaving a lecture and two patients behind."

"Well, why did you?"

He reached for the telephone. "I'll answer you both at once," he said.

"All right. I'm listening."

Jared set the phone down. "He won't be free. He's busy, and with that guy—"

"How does he stay so cheerful and—and—funny, really, with the things he does?"

"I think he worked up a strong self-defense when living with my father," said Jared. "And that's what brought me home early."

106

Her head lifted sharply.

"I do too much thinking," Jared said quietly. "Ever since he told us about his childhood. I am working and I go on working, but the pictures come. That child, my brother, but it could have been me, working himself into a man in spite of a father who didn't give a damn for him. Just as he didn't give a damn for me." He put out his hand to her. "Let me say this and don't be hurt, my darling. Why do we—why do I, at least, think so much about other people when I should think about myself, my work, my contribution to life?"

"You do."

"Not recently. Recently my work doesn't come first. I do."

"But, Jared—"

"I've been able to work, too, and do good work. But lately—"

"Before Joel told of his father's selfishness— Didn't your questions start when you thought Joel and I—?"

"I was ready to kill him, Mother. I was."

"A woman, Jared . . ."

"It wasn't you. I could forgive and understand you. But the thought of Joel—and just because I held that thought, I have been as bad as our father."

"You've not shown your thoughts. I could tell no difference. Have you talked this out with Joel?"

He smiled at her. "How wise you are," he said.

"Your shock—Brig thinks we should marry."

"Why don't you?" he asked.

"Things would change around here."

"Yes, they would. Though you'd still live here."

"I would, yes. But Joel would know that you believe—"

"Does he think I still—"

"I'm afraid he does, Jared. Since that night, he does not touch me, or kiss me when he comes into the house."

"I'm his father's son." Jared rose and went over to the window. "That is what is bothering me, Helen. That I could ever be like him."

"You're not. And there are a dozen people you're just as apt to be like. Including a very swell guy named Dr. Jared O'Brien."

"When I get angry or hurt, I let the matter get to me. I lost Lutie that way."

"You lost Joel for a short time. Now you are together again."

"Yes. But—I can't afford a temper, Mother."

"No, you can't. I'd hoped to see you restored to your affection for Joel. Quarreling with him, talking, loving your brother."

"I think I do all those things. But what I planned to tell you—I must find myself as a man myself. Not dependent on others."

"We are all dependent on others, dear. I was on you when you were a soft-armed, sweet baby, not the big, strong man you are today."

For a time he did not speak. "I came to tell you that I was leaving," he said then.

"Certainly, if that is what you want. But I will say that you are leaving for the wrong reason. I know you were shocked about Brig—"

"Only as long as I thought it was Joel."

"Joel never would . . ."

"Yes, he would, too. He's a red-blooded guy."

Jared started to leave the room, then turned sharply. "Were there . . . ?" he began, then stopped, his face flushing. "Are there other men?"

108

Helen carefully folded her sewing. "I don't consider that your affair," she said quietly.

Jared gasped.

His mother rose and came to him. "My son," she said quietly, putting her hand on his shoulders, "you are a very smart man. In some things."

"I'm not a fool in others," he said firmly.

"Not a fool. Of course not. But blind in some. Inexperienced in others. I've blamed myself that you didn't have girls. But you've let that scar blind you to life. You listen to life in music and in books. But—did you ever kiss a girl?"

He tried to pull away.

"I know what Vietnam did to you."

"You have no idea of what it did to me, Mother. When I was in Fitzgibbons Hospital and they'd patched me up enough that I knew that there was, that there had to be, a life ahead for me, I spent the days wishing I would die. At night I prayed that I would not."

"These days, it's as if I were back at Fitz . . ."

She stretched up to kiss him. "Oh, my darling . . ."

"It isn't you," he said. "It isn't Joel. He has done wonders for me."

"But it is Lutie."

He flinched and pulled away.

"She's free . . ."

"She lived with that guy, and had a child."

"She had her problems, too."

"I know, but—"

"You have spoken of marriage before this. And that's where I hope life would start for you. It starts that way for any man. A man and a woman."

"Looked at from the outside."

"Looked at as I know you have looked at it. You loved Lutie. You set her free, and she married. Did you know the man?"

"I've met him. I still loved her and it hurt."

"It does hurt. It hurts when you marry the wrong man. I knew that, and so did Lutie."

Jared stood frowning. "I think she is the only one—"

"She is, and she knows that, too."

"Does a man have to have marriage?"

She laughed. "There seems to be things your medical schools leave out."

He bent over to search her face. "Do you know," he said, "you're right. Sex and all it can mean, what it means. We are taught the anatomy but not the inner, but still physical, need. What it means, what the lack of it can mean. The men who come to me—they are struggling to find the answer."

"And you can't help them."

"I've learned only not to try."

"Up until—until lately, you've seemed happy with the way you lived. Your studies, your hard work, your trips, our family life. At least, you have seemed content."

"I was. I am."

"No, I don't think so."

"And you?"

"Like you, I've been content."

"Has Joel helped? Or . . . ?"

"He's an alley cat. No scar would inhibit him."

"He thinks it shouldn't bother you as much as it does."

"I can't help it. The thought of pressing that scar against a woman's cheek—"

"Lutie's?"

"I myself made Lutie out of the question."

"She's going to stay here with her father and the little girl."

"Maggie," said Jared softly.

"Yes. I'm not pushing you, Jared." Helen spoke softly.

"You are, but I know it. I know what will come, will come. But, lately, there's you, dear. You're still a vibrant, beautiful woman."

"In my son's eyes."

"I can't help but wonder—"

"Have there been other men?"

"Yes, that and—"

"Joel?"

Jared said nothing.

"He knows that I look at him as another son. And we both know he wouldn't have me. You come first with him."

Jared flushed. "But I don't want that!"

She touched his arm. And started to leave the room. "It's what we get in this world, my son," she said.

He stood staring at the door.

Then he turned and went back to the kitchen. "I'm going down the hill," he told Zenobia.

"Miss Lutie be glad to see you," said the black woman comfortably.

Jared walked, shaking his head. "What will be," he muttered, "is apt to be what the women want it to be."

6

The next morning when Jared came down to breakfast, Zenobia faced him at the foot of the stairs. "You done got another of them movie biggies at your hospital," she said accusingly.

He blinked.

"It's the phone, dear," said Helen from the breakfast table. She was laughing.

"And this," Joel added, handing him the newspaper, pointing to a certain item. Jared glanced at the paper,

"I forgot it was due," he said.

The item said, "Talk show headliner Paul Menamara and his bride checked in at the Parkmoor last night. Their reservations were made by Dr. Jared O'Brien's office, but I will spare some of our delicate readers a description of wherein lies Dr. O'Brien's expertise."

Jared laid the paper aside and sat down to his orange juice and hot toast. "I'm sorry," he muttered.

"I have to be away all day, dear," said Helen, turning her head toward the phone which Ivory had answered. "It keeps a strong man busy."

"Mhmnnnn. I'll send one of the secretaries out. I'm sorry."

"We can't have the telephone cut off."

"Oh, of course not."

"How about Lutie? I have to be away today, and she gets bored."

"I'll ask her, and you can brief her."

"Good. And pay her a little, too, son. She's looking for work."

"I'll stop there on my way to the city. Damn these curious wolves."

Lutie's father saw Jared's car turn in at the farm's gate, and called his daughter.

"Your beau's comin' to call," he said.

Lutie laughed. "I'm too old to have beaus," she told him, "and eight in the morning is a strange time."

But she went to the door, hearing her father say something about strange beaus.

Yes, it was Jared's cream and brown car, and Jared getting out of it. The baby saw him, too, and came flying.

Jared caught her up in his arms as the door opened. "Maggie, Maggie," he said happily.

"Come inside," laughed Lutie, brushing her bright hair back from her face. "What's happening?"

Jared kissed her cheek as he always did. "Favors," he said. "As usual."

"Granted, as usual," she told him. "Come in where Papa is. He'll want to know."

"No secrets, eh?"

"Impossible."

He followed her, loving the way her hair rippled against her shoulders. Loving every inch of this small, trim woman.

113

"Good morning, Doctor," said the man seated in the deep chair beside the open fire. "You'll excuse me."

Jared set the child beside her grandfather. "Isn't she a precious one?" he asked. "I came to borrow Lutie."

Mr. Pershall looked up sharply. "Borrow?"

"Yes. I'd like to hire her to come to our house and answer the telephone for a day or two."

"You've another famous patient," said Lutie. "Sure. I'll come. Papa will be glad to get rid of me."

"She's restless," explained Mr. Pershall.

"Oh, the newspapers got wind of a certain celebrity who desires my services. They seek publicity. I don't. I have the hospital pretty well trained, but Mother has to be away, and Zenobia and Ivory—"

Lutie had already taken her coat from the hook in the hallway. "I'll leave Maggie to take care of Grandpa," she said. Her green eyes were shining. Just to be with Jared, just to see his tall person close by, to be asked to do anything for him—

"I'll have to be getting along," he said. "Will you swap cars with me, Lutie?"

"My doodlebug for your—?" she laughed. "Any day, boy. Any day. Who's the celebrity?"

He told her and she whistled. "Dr. O'Brien is not at home, and I have no information," she rehearsed her reply to the telephone caller. "How long will this go on, Jared?"

"As long as they need to be in town. About three days, I suspect. I'll give you the hospital code number in case you have to call me."

"Oh, yes. But things will go fine. Papa loves to spoil Maggie and he'll bring her up to the house during the day."

Lutie gave him the keys to her small red car, watched him transfer his medical bag and some papers from his own. She laughed at the contrast between the cars. "I'll make this trade any day, sir," she said. "But I shall need your keys."

He snorted and gave them to her. "You're a doll," he told her. "I'll check in, as I can." He gave her a slip on which a single word was printed. The hospital's phone centers would have it, and—

He doubled his long legs to get into Lutie's little car. "The job pays twenty bucks a day," he said, starting with a jerk. She waved him on. To do anything for Jared, to live for three or four days in his beautiful home, she would not need, or take, money from him. But maybe she did need a job. At the hospital perhaps. . . . He was out of sight.

For a happy week she worked at the O'Brien home, because before the celebrity had departed, word circulated that the man whose penis Jared had reattached was back in normal condition.

"You get more risqué publicity than a porno actress," Lutie told Jared.

"Don't blame me. Tell the patients where to fall and what to cut off."

"Jared and Lutie," Mr. Pershall told Helen, "seem back to their teenage selves again."

"I wish—" sighed Helen.

"Isn't his cheek much better?"

"Yes, it is, but his problem is that he told her he could not marry her."

"Way back at the beginning of the war."

"I know. I hope she doesn't get tired of his excuse and find herself another man."

"She won't. She told me that marriage without love was a horror."

"Yes, it would be. Does she like her new job at the hospital?"

"Oh, yes. But if Maggie has the sniffles I have a hard time convincing her that I know how to take care of the child."

Helen smiled and nodded, "They don't grow up, and they won't be convinced that we learn a few things, too."

It turned out to be a quiet winter. The two doctors were busy, but no extraordinary crisis developed. Along after Christmas, Helen married Brig. A thing Jared approved and urged his mother to do. But would she travel with him? They had gone to the West Indies for a honeymoon.

"Suppose you let Miss Helen do the deciding," Zenobia advised him, "She ain't give up lovin' you and this house."

Of course not. But Joel decided to take an apartment close to the hospital. Maybe Jared would join him?

"I'll see how things are when Helen gets back."

"Is the House yours or hers?"

Jared frowned. "What difference does that make?"

"Oh, I was thinking of wills and things."

"Cheerful subject."

"I like it."

"The House is mine. But what is mine is Helen's, and it always will be."

"When are you going to marry Lutie?"

"When you learn to keep your big mouth shut," said Jared.

"You'll both be white-headed," Joel answered amiably, getting up to see what had set his beeper off.

"Guess what?" he asked Jared, who was still reading.

"We both should have been preachers," Jared told him, which was a recurring joke between them. "I wish you'd come back here to live."

116

"I wish I'd had the sense enough to stay in my little home sweet home tonight," said Joel, turning up the collar of his raincoat. "This promises to be a hassle between me and the medical examiner."

"Because you won't let him do his job."

"Because he doesn't always do his job," Joel said over his shoulder, going out through the kitchen to tell Ivory he was leaving in case any calls came there.

"I'll be at the hospital or my apartment," he told the tall man.

"My mom wants to know if you keep clean socks. She wants me to look in—"

"Tell her to look in herself," said Joel. "Lots of the girls go to see the boys these days."

He left Ivory convulsed with laughter.

Joel, doing traumatic surgery, occasionally did have differences with the medical examiner. And Joel could be an irritating antagonist. The medical examiner did not relish being called mistaken in his verdicts, and Joel did not like being called "Quincy." Both of which circumstances did not make for peace over certain deaths or victims already dead who had contact with the hospital emergency rooms.

That night was a typical experience, and Joel knew he was in for a night and possibly days of argument over a court experience, certainly days of reports of all sorts. "Who told me to go into trauma," he asked when he came back to change his raincoat for an overcoat. It was cold outside, he'd discovered.

"You talked yourself into it," Jared assured him.

"Want to come along?"

"I might. What's happened?"

"Oh, this fella, a convicted killer already, went around

117

shouting things like 'I'm God and he's the devil,' and the other day—yesterday in fact—he stabbed a workman on a street corner with a twelve-inch butcher knife. And now he's dead himself after battling the police, who were ready and prepared in battle gear. Now I'm expected to decide whether the officers acted properly."

By this time Jared was in the car seat beside him and they were driving as swiftly as they could into the city, to the hospital.

"It seems this fellow was on parole granted about four years ago after spending some time for murder in a hospital for the criminally insane."

"Have you seen him?"

"Oh, yes. They brought him to emergency. The fellow was pretty well scratched up. I say he died of traumatic asphyxiation. The medical examiner ruled the death accidental."

"And . . . ?"

"I surveyed the man's body. It indicated that the guy had died of traumatic asphyxiation caused by pressure on the chest while the police were trying to subdue him. The man he had stabbed died fifteen minutes later."

"At our hospital?"

"Yes. Whoever did the chart record said that the killer had a knife and kept singing something about his being God and the other fellow was the devil. The police were called and he kept on screaming nonsense and slashing in circles."

"How did they, the police, subdue him?"

"I told you. They ganged him. Well, they brought in the F.D. and—"

"The what?" asked Jared, shifting in his seat.

118

"Oh, you damned innocent. No, you bury your head in the O.R. and—"

"Far from that," laughed Jared.

Joel laughed, too. "I never have asked you what you did with that celebrity who kept us all tied in knots for a week."

"And I never told you. How—?"

"They brought in the Fire Department, dear, innocent brother. They had flailed at him with clubs and stuff. The television account shows that. But finally the knife was knocked from his hand by heavy hose spray. This disarmed him, and they brought him to the hospital."

"Dead?"

"Unconscious. Forty-five minutes later he was dead. I almost declared that he was drowned. I never saw a wetter patient. I say he died of the bruises and injuries inflicted by the police clubs and the fire-hose spray."

"Why did they need an autopsy?"

"I asked for one and got it."

"That's what you're going to do now?"

"Sure it is. If I can prove his chest was so beaten and—"

"Traumatized," murmured Jared.

"I should have left you at home."

Joel pulled the car up the ramp and slid it into its slot of the parking space.

"You won't win this," said Jared.

"I know it. But I keep these guys on their toes. Every DOA that comes to the emergency room does *not* die of natural causes."

"You have to take me home—"

Joel rattled his keys. "Take my car home and bring it or the keys back in the morning. This autopsy—"

"You'll walk home?"

119

"To my apartment? Sure. I'll get one of the nurses to go with me for protection."

"She'd go, too," Jared said, laughing. "Can't I stay around for a time?"

"Certainly. Sign in, though. We don't need both of us up before the board."

When he finally went home, Jared told Helen and Brig briefly why they had gone to the hospital. Brig said Joel should write a book about such cases.

Jared and Helen both laughed.

"Why wouldn't he?"

"He should, but he gets so many of them."

"Then you, Jared, should write one about the celebrities you've restored to fertility," said Brig.

Jared too had seen the articles in the newspapers. But Brig's suggestion angered him. He never used his profession, he said coldly.

"Except in a scientific way and terms," said Helen quietly. "Are you working on a book, dear?"

Jared shook his head. "I'm trying to learn to be more social."

"That's where you go these nights?"

"About once a month won't do it," Brig assured his wife's son. "I hear Joel has a live-in friend."

Jared said nothing.

"Do you know her?" Helen asked Jared.

"Brig started that story. Let him finish it."

Brig laughed. And watched Jared go into the hall, heard him go upstairs.

"What's wrong with Jared these days?" he asked Helen.

She shook her head. "Whatever it is, he seems to be forgetting his face."

"Isn't it better?"

120

"He forgets the scar at times and often doesn't wear the mask. Joel's been working on his discarding that. And Sunday, if you noticed, he didn't wear it when he read the lessons."

Brig shook his head. "He's a funny chap," he said thoughtfully.

Helen's head lifted, and he made a brushing motion with his hands. "I know he's perfect," he assured Jared's mother.

"I wish Joel had stayed here."

"He couldn't have a live-in friend here."

"He never seemed to miss one here."

"Tell me, Helen. Is Jared's face better? Healing, I mean."

"I don't think it is, or ever will be. For years it's been the mental, the inside-of-himself scar that was doing the damage."

Brig's red cheeks turned a brighter crimson. "I am not in any way a psychiatrist, Helen, dear. . . ," he said diffidently.

She smiled at him. "He's gone the route with psychiatry and analysis, dear."

"Then maybe he himself . . . "

"With Joel's help."

"Yes. You know? Joel is a remarkable chap. The newspaper article about this case mentioned their father."

"I know it did, and both of the boys were angry. Actually, what difference does it make? Their work in medicine is good and they've done it on their own. Their father was so only by happenstance."

Brig repeated the word. He was a quiet man, sturdy, not especially handsome, but his military past showed in his erect, firm body, his constant cleanliness, his observance of

121

every rule of courtesy. Brig was a man to like, and people did like him. "I can't see," Joel once said to Helen, "why you didn't marry him and have some decent kids of your own."

Helen had flushed. "Brig was afraid of the money Jared's grandfather had left us."

Jared protested. "You always said—"

"I know what I said. That Brig wants to travel. I want to take care of my house and my son. Sons."

"Me, too?" asked Joel, surprised. He had come out for a Sunday afternoon. He looked tired, and Helen had already spoken of her concern for him.

"Don't worry about me. Let's get old Jared straightened out. He'd doing marvelous work at the hospital, incidentally. Have you ever seen him work, Helen?"

"No, dear. I've read the articles printed about him, listened to people praise him. But the nature of his surgery—For that matter, I've never seen you work."

Joel laughed. "It's too rough and tumble."

"Yes, I know. But—Joel, I am about convinced that Jared's scar no longer gives him an excuse—"

"I know. He hides behind it and I plan to tell him so."

"You don't think the scar has been a hindrance for some time, do you?"

"Well—"

"The trouble now is down the hill, isn't it?"

"Lutie. Yes."

"He sees a lot of her, pretending it's Maggie who calls on his attention."

"Maggie helps. But the guy is so damn stubborn."

"Is he really?"

"Yes, he is, Helen. He has established a way of life, and

122

loss of Lutie is a big part of it. He wouldn't know what to do if he didn't have that loss to hide behind."

Helen regarded him thoughtfully. "You are a very smart man, Joel O'Brien," she said.

"Time will tell how smart I am. I think I'll go down and take Jared's girl away from him."

"Can you?"

"Oh, sure. I'm death on three-year-olds."

Helen watched him from the windows. He strode down the grassy slope, pulling his jacket collar up behind his ears. He should have worn an overcoat or wrap of some kind. There was a stiff wind blowing.

He caught up with Jared and the pony, with Maggie on its back.

Brig joined her at the window. They watched the picture made by the two tall men, the pony, and the little girl with her blowing red curls.

"Don't other men see Lutie for what she is?" Brig asked.

"They do, and sometimes I'm afraid that Joel will step in."

"Oh, he wouldn't!"

"Why wouldn't he? Brothers have done that sort of thing often enough before this."

"I think Lutie is in love with Jared."

"I think she always has been. But when he sent her word from Vietnam that she should not wait for him— He'd been wounded and was in no condition to marry. He was terribly banged up, but Lutie took it to mean that he didn't want her, and she married one of the men who were always available to her. She was very young—"

She broke off and started for the door. Brig caught her arm.

"They're not watching that baby," cried Helen. "She's going to get her feet wet, if nothing worse."

"They won't allow that," said Brig, not sounding too certain. They pony had drifted back to the farm and his stable. Jared and Joel were talking earnestly. Maggie had been left to amuse herself.

"They don't quarrel very often" said Helen, " but I do believe—"

"Get your coat then, and rescue Maggie," said Brig.

Joel and Jared were talking intently, arguing, then quarreling . . .

About women. About Lutie in particular. Joel was warning Jared, as Helen was prepared to do, that other men . . .

Jared did not appreciate Joel's telling him what to do.

"You've made a beautiful mess of your sex life so far," said Joel roughly.

"All right. I lost Lutie," Jared agreed. "And I grant you that I stay clear of the ladies . . ."

"That isn't the way to get your bed warm."

Jared shook his head. "Don't talk that way," he said. "It's cheap."

Joel laughed. "You lean on that damn scar. You talk pretty to the girls, and you put a double bed up in your room. Then nothing happens."

"Does it have to?"

"How old are you, brother? Do you ever get talked about at the hospital in the girl department?"

"You get enough talk there to make up for both of us."

"All right. I like the ladies."

"I like them, but—"

"You've got that damn scar. Good God, man, we all got 'em at Nam. Yours just shows."

Jared opened his mouth to speak, then turned to find

124

Maggie instead. Joel had spoken the truth. And it was time— He would pick up the child and go in search of Lutie, and tell her—

But Helen got to Maggie first. "You've let her get her feet wet," she said accusingly. "I'll take her up to the house."

"I'll do it, Helen," said Jared.

"Where's the pony? He was your responsibility, too."

"I'm going back to the city," said Joel.

"Oh, Joel, dear—"

"Your son isn't very good company," said Joel, walking up to the house.

"What were you two talking about?" Helen asked when Jared took the heavy child from her arms.

"Joel thinks I should marry Lutie."

"So do I."

Jared stared at her. "But—"

"You still have the scar. She never sees it. If you'd do what we all want, you really would go down there now, with Maggie, get her into dry clothes, and tell Lutie—"

And Jared's beeper went off. Joel was signaling from the House. "There's been a fire at the hospital," he called.

Jared gave Maggie to Helen and sprinted up the hill. A fire at the hospital—

The patients—the instruments—he ran harder.

7

The fire did no great damage, but the fire drill had the patients upset. Neither Joel nor Jared came home for the evening meal. Helen heard Jared come in very late.

The next day he said he had a trip to make.

"Speaking?"

"Listening. There's a chap from Australia showing a new technique."

"In your field?"

"Neurosurgery. Yes."

"Did Ivory pack your bag?"

"I did."

"Then let me check. Remember the time you forgot socks."

"You've not let me forget them since." But he laughed, and opened his bag.

"Helen?" he asked. The tone of his voice made her look around.

"What is it, dear?"

"Do you think I do the wrong thing, staying here in your way and Brig's, not having my own apartment?"

"No, not unless you want one at the hospital."

126

"Not to bring a girl home to. *Whee-hoo!* Would that raise a stink!"

Helen laughed. "Is it true that nice gi·ls . . .?

"Of course it's true. Joel seems happy enough."

"Yes, he does."

"Zenobia might have a fit, but when I come back I think I'll ask them both out for Sunday dinner."

"Zenobia will think it's a sign that Joel is planning to get married."

"Not if I tell her . . ."

"Then don't tell her," said Helen sensibly.

Halfway down the stairs, Jared stopped. "Mother . . .?" he asked.

"Brig's good for me. He has taught me, shown me things I never had with your father, and have only guessed at since."

"Then good for Brig! I'm glad you won't be lonesome, dear. You can reach me through the office. Take care."

As it happened, Jared came home as usual, unannounced, the Sunday afternoon when Helen had asked Joel to bring his girlfriend out for supper. Lutie just happened to drop in that same afternoon, and was asked to stay.

She looked down at her blouse and skirt. She had the knack of always looking trim and pretty. The other girl was more dressy. She was a blonde with her thick hair smoothed across her brow, back over her head.

"How does she keep it that way?" Lutie whispered to Helen.

"We could ask her. She is pretty, too. She has both Joel and Brig interested in her."

"Is she the one . . .?"

"We could ask her that, too," said Helen, and Lutie giggled.

127

And it was just at that point that Ivory brought Jared's bags, followed by Jared himself through the side door. He had telephoned from the airport.

He was happy to be home, and showed it. He glanced around as if checking on each well-loved item of his house. He glanced at the people seated around the fire. He went over and kissed Helen, turned and kissed Lutie, "Like a sister," Joel angrily told him later. Then he turned to the young blond woman who was sitting on the loveseat with Joel, the light from the window very pretty upon her hair.

Jared took two long steps toward her. "Hello, Marie!" he said heartily. "How nice to find you here." He bent to kiss her, and Joel decided to stand up, defeating his purpose.

"I know she's your girl," Jared told him, "but I kiss all the ladies."

He did not. Helen always. Lutie sometimes. Other girls, never.

"If you'll excuse me . . ." he said, "I'll go freshen up. I flew all night, got bumped at Philadelphia, had to change in Chicago . . ."

Still talking, he was out of the room.

"Do I know him?" Marie asked Joel.

"You do now," he grumbled. "Lutie is his girl."

Both Lutie and Helen laughed. "When they were three and six, we would have all agreed with you, Joel," Helen told him. "She is the girl next door," she apologized to their visitor.

"He's very handsome," murmured Marie, watching the doorway through which Jared had disappeared.

Jared came down quickly, wearing a white turtleneck sweater and blue flannel slacks. Marie was still seated beside Joel, but flirting with Brig. Helen had left the room to see about supper. At Jared's entry, Marie came and tucked her hand into his elbow. "I want you to tell me what all these lovely things are," she told him earnestly. "Is the house very old?"

Lutie went out to the kitchen. "I've never seen Jared act this way before," she told Zenobia and Helen.

"She's devlin' Dr. Joel," said Zenobia, not looking up from the biscuits she was rolling.

"Oh," said Lutie, "I thought it might be me."

Helen laughed. "Pay it no mind," she said. "Joel isn't."

But Brig was, and so was Joel after a little of it. Dinner was delicious, as always, and Lutie watched the girl, Marie, flirt with Jared. Girls often did that, and he managed to leave the scene, but tonight he stayed on, seated across from Marie, leaning forward to talk to her.

Helen was puzzled. He had never done that before. Was she the live-in girlfriend of Joel? If so—

Joel ate his dinner and scarcely spoke, until Marie called Brig "Mr. Morse."

Then his big, strong hand fell on her shoulder. "It's General Morse, sweetheart," he said firmly. "You're going to have to learn about these things."

"Mr. Brig Morse?" she asked, wide-eyed. She had lovely violet eyes.

"No, dear," said Helen, above the laughter. "His full title is Brigadier General Morse, Retired, United States Marine Corps."

"Oh," said Marie. "And you just call him Brig for short."

"The girl has brains," drawled Jared, and Joel flared. Helen signaled to the kitchen that they were ready for dessert. She had seen the anger in Joel's eyes. But he wouldn't— He surely would not—

But he almost did. "Tell us, Dr. Jared O'Brien," he said, "what you've been seeing and doing on your travels."

Jared rested his chin on his hands. "I'll take a fiver not to say one word," he said.

Lutie stepped in, "Now you two boys quit!" she said firmly. "Eat your lime cream pie, wipe the meringue off your beard, and we'll play Monopoly."

This brought them to a realization of what they were about to do. Joel and Jared often argued, and hotly, but tonight was different. Marie even ventured to ask Jared what the patch was that he wore. No one ever mentioned that patch. And of course no one ever touched it. But Marie seemed ready to do both, and both Lutie and Joel stopped her.

"I'm sorry," said the poor girl. She had not expected such heat, such—

Helen patted her hand. "It's a war scar, my dear," she said softly.

But Joel's voice overrode her. "It's a hole in his head," he said roughly. "Didn't you guess he had one?"

Jared was on his feet; Joel rose to face him, both men white with anger.

Brig shouted at them to sit down, and Helen was saying something about Vietnam.

"Yes!" Joel caught at the word. "He got it in Vietnam. He loves it and cherishes it. Leans on it. But we all got scars there. Ours don't show, perhaps. But he leans on his. He's a dramatic genius with that damn scar. It shows, ours don't."

The words tumbled over each other. Jared went around the table, Helen clutching at his sweater.

But Jared was about to put his hand on Joel's shoulder. "You're right," he said. "And I am sorry."

But Joel was not to be appeased. "I'm leaving the hospital," he said angrily.

"You are not! It was all right for you to leave the House,

but you are needed at the hospital. Now, do as Lutie says."

Joel made an involuntary gesture to his mouth, and they all laughed.

There was no Monopoly game. Immediately after coffee, Jared said he was tired and would go up to bed. Would his mother excuse him?

"And me, too," said Joel, smoothly.

"Well, you won't let me talk about my trip, and you don't think Vietnam is a proper subject, so what else is there to do?" He went over and kissed Marie's cheek. "Good night, sweetheart. I'm sorry Joel met you first."

He left an uncomfortable silence in the room, which extended into their lives for the next few days. Joel did not come back to the House. Maggie developed chicken pox, and Lutie stayed away. Jared came and went as usual, leaving early in the morning, returning for a somewhat stiff dinner, then going to his rooms.

"Did he and Joel make up?" Brig asked Helen.

"Oh, they surely did. They are both very busy."

"Joel doesn't care a whoop for that girl."

"Which she knows. What she'd like would be for Jared to care for her."

"He won't."

"No, and I'm glad for that."

Maggie got better, and Lutie brought her up to the House. "Are those two boys still mad at each other?" she asked Helen.

"They never were mad, dear. Jared is sensitive about his face . . . "

"He's better than he used to be. I think Joel devils him into speaking of it sometimes."

"Yes, but I don't like him to spoil what should be a pleasant evening. I think I'll talk to Joel."

"Hasn't he been around?" Lutie was surprised.

131

"He hasn't been back since Sunday. But he's very busy."

"You might call him."

"I was going to, anyway. Brig and I are going on a short cruise to the Bahamas. I want to tell the boys."

She did call Joel, and had to leave her name for him to call back. He said he was sorry; his manners were terrible. The lime cream pie deserved better.

She mentioned the trip. "I'd like to see you before we leave. We miss you around here."

He made no comment.

"Now, Joel—"

"When can you come in for dinner with me?"

"You won't cook it."

"Oh, no! That's a promise. But I'd like to hold up my end."

"Are you inviting Jared?"

"Just you and Brig."

"I know what you are trying to do for Jared."

"So does he. That's the trouble. Can I come out late this afternoon and maybe stay for dinner?"

"Come any time you like. Zenobia has red beans cooked."

"*Whoopee!* I'll be there. And I'll check my brother's schedule before I come."

"Joel—"

He had hung up.

And when he did come he had a wonderful black eye.

Brig whistled. Helen softly touched her handkerchief to his cheek.

"Jared didn't do it," Joel hastened to say. "I had a patient that got out of hand. And that was a funny one, too, because I had to call Jared in to see if he could help the man. He was afraid he would lose his vital statistics."

"Was Jared nice to you?"

"Now, Mother-Helen—"

"I know, I know," she apologized. "I've often wondered how you two could work together when you feel—"

"I like Jared."

"And he likes you. But you do get into these conflicts, dear. Why?"

"We're jealous because he has you and I don't. He also has Lutie—"

Helen's head lifted. "Lutie?"

"He doesn't know it, and you don't. But Lutie does."

"Then why in hell," said Brig, "doesn't the girl chase him?"

"Haven't you seen girls—women—chase Jared?"

"In the hospital, you mean?" asked Brig.

"There, and in church. He's a porcupine. He senses what they are doing. And he says doctors make bad husbands."

Joel broke off to consider what he had said. "I suppose they do," he conceded. "For a dozen reasons. They can keep any hours they like. Four women out of five get silly about their doctor."

"Jared doesn't have many women patients, does he?"

"He has some. And his other patients have wives."

Helen nodded.

"And you're too good to him. You provide him with a home no young wife could approach."

"This home belongs to Jared."

"He'd never take it away from you."

"I'd leave. For the right girl."

"Where do you find the right girl?"

"Next door."

"But the guy's so damn bull-headed—"

"I know."

"Where is he these days?"

"You saw him this afternoon. But you're right. He did go away the day after we had lime cream pie. He went on a lecture tour."

"Yes, I know that. Lasted about four days. He hates this kind of lecturing. He doesn't mind doing it to professionals, but when he is faced with a bunch of clubwomen, or some such assemblage, and has to explain . . . " Joel stood up and thrust his hands into his trouser pockets.

"When you do that you look like Jared," said Helen, laughing.

"I know I do and it makes him furious to have people say so."

"Go on with what you were saying," said Brig. "I've never heard Jared lecture."

"Well, let's see." Joel struck his pose again. "A vasectomy," he said, dropping his voice to the register of Jared's, "can be used as a birth control device. It saves the little wife from worry with IUD's and pills, and the fear of an accidental motherhood. I use the word 'wife' freely, you understand. It is not a painful operation; the whole process is done in an hour, and performed in the doctor's office. Under a local anesthetic there is no pain, and healing is without incident.

"O.K! But the man divorces his wife, or whatever." Joel's eyes glinted. "And the patient meets and perhaps marries a girl who wants children. He hears about Jared, not his charges but his ability. Jared examines him and decides he is a proper subject, which he is if the vasectomy was done properly. The prospective father goes to the hospital, the surgery takes three or four hours, under anesthesia, and you never saw a woman do as delicate, patient handiwork. He is a joy to watch."

Helen nodded. "I know that. I've heard other doctors talk about his delicate handiwork."

"It *is* delicate and he has improved on the usual instruments. He is quite famous, you know."

Brig laughed. "You're talking to the fella's mother," he reminded Joel.

"I knew that. Old Jared's written another book, you know."

"This is supposed to be for laymen, and it deals with all sorts of microsurgery." Helen spoke proudly.

"And he's been asked to appear on some talk shows."

"Which he won't do," said Helen confidently.

"Well, as it happens, I think he is going to do it. He's a fan of one of the hosts."

"Jared was never a fan of anybody," said Brig

"Oh, now—"

"Well, he does have some favorite musicians. But he isn't a *fan*. This woman got to know him when he was in the army hospital."

"An old lady," said Helen dryly.

"She is not. Besides, he wants to plug his book. He says it answers all the dumb-fool questions women—wives, usually—ask him."

"I ask him some he won't answer. That is, he evades answering. Will he be on TV?"

"Yes, with his face in the correct profile."

"Why hasn't he told me?"

"He may not want his friends to watch. The hospital hasn't announced it, though the matter has leaked out."

"Does Lutie know?"

"She will if you tell her."

Helen laughed, rather bitterly. "I had so hoped—"

"So has Lutie."

"Will he be gone long?"

135

"I know his work schedule is blank for three weeks. He's going to England, he told me."

"Yes. He told me that much. But three weeks—"

"He'll do three talk shows here."

"In California. He asked Zenobia about his lightweight suits."

"You'd never know he was on speaking terms with his family."

But Helen never liked to have Jared criticized, and contented herself with saying that he would tell her before he left.

Which he did.

"Why are you going to England?" she asked him.

"That's for a church meeting, Mother. It will be in the papers."

She regarded him bravely. "I've known you for much longer," she said, "than I did your father. But do all men treat women like idiots?"

"Brig doesn't treat you like an idiot."

She had come up to his room, where he was packing two bags. "Do one warm clothes, the other light," she advised.

He nodded, and began to shift garments. She noted the church vestments in a cellophane container. His church obligations pleased her. Nothing made her more proud than to see him stand and perform the rites of their church. But why must he be secretive?

She sat down in the rocking chair. "I wish you would talk to me," she said.

"Joel tells you everything I do."

"Yes, and I thank him for it. But these blank spaces in your life— They are like your father, and they frighten me."

He looked contrite. "I'm sorry."

"I don't want to *live* your life, but, especially since Joel has been around, you do withdraw. We all notice it. Zenobia, Brig, Lutie—"

He continued to work on the one suitcase, closed it, snapped it. Then he came to kneel beside Helen. "I love you more than anyone I could ever know," he said gravely. "But I was to blame for my hurt from Lutie. I don't want to have you hurt me."

Her fingers gently crept up to the scar on his cheek. "I wish you could forget that, dear."

"I never can. You—and Lutie—have to know that I cannot. But—you're right. I have stepped aside for Joel. He has so much fun, he is so free and open—and he's never been hurt."

"Oh, yes, he has, my son. Because he lived with your father a great many years."

Jared fell back upon his heels. "Did he tell you?"

"He doesn't. He has never had to tell me."

Jared stood up. "I think every hurt has to show," he muttered. "But you're right, dear. You know, he didn't hunt me out at the hospital, though he did come there for a job. Because of me. Well—all right. I'll try to persuade him to come back to the House and I'll give him the schedule. My talk shows are in Los Angeles—Burbank, really—Chicago and New York. Then I am going to be in New York and England because of the church meeting. And because there is a doctor, a microneurologist who has done some amazing things with the cornea of the eyes. She wants to see how I work. I am more interested in her and what she does. And if this household wants to work on a romance, she is in her early thirties."

Helen laughed.

8

Jared did go to England. Previously Helen had caught him on three talk shows. He talked a little about his book, and then the master of ceremonies took over, and one of the guests cooked, drawing Jared into the project. Zenobia and Helen laughed.

"He used to help us make cookies," Helen reminded their cook. "Why should she suppose—"

"I don't think that will sell a book," decided Brig.

Helen and Zenobia agreed with him, and Jared did not appear on the final program. There was some excuse, a delayed plane, Helen told Joel, who asked for a report.

"He didn't want to do it, though he talks more than well."

"And is continually aware of his cheek."

"He was successful in California and Chicago. His secretary says they have bags of mail forwarded to his office here."

"Do you think he will read it?"

"Patients have piled up still more thickly."

"Oh, dear. I hope he enjoys England."

138

"A lot depends on this woman surgeon. If she strikes the right note. She won't be concerned with his face."

"No, she won't."

And no, she was not. She looked at him in some surprise. "What happened to you?" she asked directly.

Involuntarily his hand went to his cheek.

"I've seen pictures of you," she insisted. "I knew you were young, but—"

"You're younger," he countered, and she smiled at the skill with which he avoided the first question.

"You're sensitive about it, but really it makes your face more attractive."

"I'd settle for its being less beautiful," he told her.

"Yes, I daresay you would. Now tell me about your work."

"I came all the way over here to be told about yours, and to see you work. I've never attempted the eye."

"But you specialized—"

"Yes. In microsurgery. But so often it is needed in the eye. I have a brother who does traumatic surgery, and often he suggests . . ."

"I am working tomorrow, and you can see what it is I do. Scrub if you like."

"I'll observe first."

"And then I'll set up the series we secured for you to do."

So they worked together, or one observing the other, and talked about the cases afterward. Jared took her out to dinner and they talked surgery. He measured her hand against his own. She was a slender woman, but tall, and her fingers were almost as long as his. But not as blunt, or strong.

"I suppose you could reattach a limb that was torn off," she agreed.

"Perhaps."

"I read it in a medical magazine. You are a famous man, Dr. O'Brien."

They saw a lot of each other. She was something like Helen in that she was tall and had a quiet manner. Her hair was dark, and cut like a boy's. She attended the church service that he conducted, and asked about his work in the church. He spent a weekend at her home; her father helped her machine the instruments she wanted but had not the skill or knowledge of "hard stuff," as she called the chrome steel, to do the work itself. Jared worked well with the old gentleman and talked about his home. They laughed about his friends who liked cupids and those who didn't.

"If my mother invites you, would you come to America and see my setup?" he asked Dr. Eckman. "I work out of a huge hospital complex, you know."

"I've seen those on film. I think I would be frightened."

"No need. You have your own corner, or wards."

"And have to lecture in a large medical school."

He agreed. "But no need to be frightened there either. You know more than the people on the benches."

He did some work on eye cornea transplants, working with animals. "I believe," he said, "that I am better in my own field, which you won't try."

"Not unless circumstances force me."

He took her to dinner, he took her dancing. She was handsome in pale green chiffon and rich brown silk. He liked her very much, and on departure secured her promise to visit his hospital and home.

"Your home?"

"My mother, my stepfather, my half brother, a

domineering cook-housekeeper, and a handyman who takes care of us all."

"No wife?"

"Oh, no. But you'll like this half brother, who is handsomer than I am."

"But not so clever."

"I've never told him so."

That evening he kissed her when he left her at her apartment door, and the next morning he flew back to America. He told his family all about his trip. "I like the English way of speaking. They don't get sloppy the way we do."

"The cockneys . . . ," Brig attempted.

"Oh, yes. But not the middle class who have been to a school. And certainly not the educated Britisher. It's clean cut—"

"You did all right, I am sure."

"I've had a good education, and I've had a good family background and profession. But listen to me. I say 'I've instead of 'I have.'"

"We understand you."

"Why did you leave so suddenly?" Helen asked.

"I was afraid I was falling in love with the woman."

"What if you were?"

"I don't know what. That was the problem. I want to continue my work. I went over there to demonstrate, and I had done it. Falling in love was not a part of it."

Nobody said anything. Finally, Helen said, "I'll write to her."

Jared looked relieved. "Thank you, dear. And invite her father too. We talked about this house. He was amazed to find there was such a place in the States."

141

Joel snorted. "Did you see her work?"

"I did. She's very good. Maybe I could learn to do the eye."

"You'd better catch up on your waiting line before you try," Joel advised.

But Helen wrote her letter, thanking Deborah for being kind to Jared beyond the call of their profession, and inviting her and her father to come to America, see "Jared's hospital," and be their guests for a weekend, or longer if so inclined.

Dr. Eckman replied at once, and said that she and her father would make a trip to America on their "holiday," which they always shared. And yes, they would come to their city and accept the invitation to their home. Dr. O'Brien had intrigued them with his descriptions of the House.

Joel said he would move out and suggested that Jared might too. "Give them the third floor."

This could be done. Jared saw agreement in his mother's glance to Brig. But it was not his idea of the visit.

"I'll stay here," he said firmly. "Joel is the one to pick up his razor and extra shoelaces—"

"I am here by invitation!" Joel reminded him. And Helen was amazed to see that he was angry about Jared's suggestion.

The telephone broke up the discussion and Helen said that she would write to Deborah and confirm the visit. "We have plenty of room on the second floor," she reminded the men. Joel and Jared could both stay on the third floor.

"But he isn't bringing his girl into my sphere," Joel drawled. "I could take her away from him. She must know too many microsurgeons as it is."

Jared flared at this, and Helen had to stop Joel's taunting. She knew what he was up to. Once defended, Jared's interest in the young woman would be intensified.

"We both know that Jared should marry," she told Joel later. "But not until he really wants to."

"You don't think this woman . . ."

"I don't believe he would have left early if he really was interested."

"My idea was to get him interested. A little competition . . ."

"Are you sure she is right for him?"

"I think Lutie is the right one, but that seems permanently impossible. And Jared needs a woman in his bed."

"Joel doesn't?" Helen asked quietly, not looking up from the pansies she was transplanting.

"Joel takes care of that in his own way."

Helen sat back on the grass. "Why haven't you married?" she asked bluntly. "Was it your father and mother . . . ?"

"And their unwanted child." His eyes never left her face.

"I'm sorry," she said. "But—"

"Yes, I should get over it. And I almost have, a time or two. And was glad later that nothing came of it. If I could find a girl like you, Helen . . ."

"You could fear that you would treat her as your father did me."

"He hurt a lot of people, sweetheart."

"I know he did. Jared's grandparents were here to help him and me. And you are not much like the bishop."

"Thank God for that. What made Jared decide to move to hospital quarters?"

"Time, he says. His work has piled up, and he wants free time for Deborah if she comes. If he is interested in her."

143

"What if I am, too?"

She smiled at the glint in his eye. "You fall in love with all of the girls," she reminded him.

He grinned and helped her clean up the mess left on the walk by the pansy bed. "Old Jared," he said, "is working like the devil."

"His book has done well. And he always has patients on a waiting list. But I miss him."

"Darn his hide, I do, too. He really is a swell guy, Mrs. Morse."

Helen knew this. She knew that Jared did not really enjoy living in quarters. "I think I'll tell him to come home."

"He may not do it. He has an item a bit outside his work."

Helen looked up, frowning.

"Do you know a Miss Terry, dear?" Joel asked.

Helen looked bewildered. "But with Dr. Eckman coming—"

"He'll adjust himself to that, and his affairs. He wants me to move out."

"Did he ask you?"

"Oh, no. He wouldn't. He is very protective of me."
Helen laughed.

"But he is," Joel insisted. "He thinks he is somewhat responsible for me."

"For heaven's sake, why?"

"I think old Jared's sorry for me."

"Why?"

"Because of the bishop."

"Oh, dear, yes. And I started all this by thinking him wonderful." She stood, dreamy.

Joel started for the house.

"He gave me two fine sons," said Helen at his shoulder.

"I'm not always so fine."

"You are, too. You—"

"Helen, let's talk about something else."

"What?"

"Oh, what we'll feed the Eckmans. What—"

His beeper buzzed, and he swore, slowly, clearly.

She offered to carry the things in his arms. "I'll dump them in the garage," he said, "and use Ivory's phone." He began to walk very fast.

"If you have to go to the hospital, wash your face. It has pansy dust on it."

Laughing, he went into the garage, and she turned toward the house. Five minutes later, his car came around the drive. He slowed and Helen came out on the porch.

"Do you know people named Taussig?" he asked her.

"Oh, dear, yes. She was—Miss Taussig was a nurse at the hospital. She's been retired for a number of years."

"Our boy has been asked by the estate—"

"What estate?"

"This woman—a Miss Taussig—"

"That's the one," said Helen. "But she must be—"

"Ninety-three years old."

Helen stood, frowning. "Why . . . ?"

"Well, it seems she has died. And the police said she had named Jared to be her executor—"

Helen nodded. "She was fond of him when he was studying medicine. She cried when he was wounded. I'm going with you."

"Now, Helen—"

"Jared will be glad to have me." She went into the house.

Joel could hear her talking to Zenobia. Then she came out with a light coat over the dress she was wearing. "Jared won't need us both," he said.

"If he needs you, he needs me. If not, I'll get myself home. He was very fond of Taussig."

"Did you know her?"

"Of course I knew her. She worked at the hospital for years and years. Considered a little on the queer side, but she was wonderful, really. She loved Jared as a medical student, she cried when he went to Vietnam, and came to see me in the middle of the night when word came that he'd been wounded. It was the end of her shift."

Joel made a gruff sound in his throat.

"She encouraged him to specialize in microsurgery. She—well—Has she really died?"

"If one needs an executor, dear—"

"Yes. When she retired—that's some time ago, of course—she went to live with her brother and sister.

"I believe they have died, too. There was something odd about that—at the time. One of them died, and she said he, or she, was to be buried in Indiana. But she wanted the undertaker to hold the body for three or four days, and the other one did die. Then the two bodies were taken to Indiana."

"Did Taussig go?"

"I don't know. But the hospital talked about the matter and wondered how she knew the sister, or whatever, would die within four days."

"She was an excellent nurse, you said."

"Oh, she was!"

"Did you go to see her? When the brother and sister died."

"I called, but the phone had been disconnected. And I

146

understand that no one has seen her since. She goes to a nearby food store and returns home, but no one goes in the house."

"And now she's dead."

"It would seem so. There's Jared's car."

Joel pulled up behind it, and he and Helen got out. Jared was waiting at the front door. "He looks shocked," whispered Joel in Helen's ear. "Maybe you should wait in the car."

She shook her head; she also said "No" to Jared's suggestion.

"There is something odd here, Helen," he said softly. "The lawyer chap is to meet me. Us."

The "lawyer chap" arrived within minutes. He held a chain with three keys. The house was a small, neat one in the center of a neat lawn.

"The neighbors say she cut the grass at night," said the lawyer.

"Why?"

"She didn't talk to or see anyone. She went out once a month for groceries. She—" He unlocked the door. "Mrs. O'Brien," he said tentatively. "Perhaps you should—"

"She's going in," Jared told him. "What's happened here?"

"The hospital is the residual heir and you are the executor," said the lawyer. He pushed the door open. And the four people went in. Into an entirely empty house, shades drawn, no furniture, except the kitchen stove, a refrigerator, and a chair. Nothing else. Nothing.

Jared moved to the other rooms. All were empty. In the smaller bedroom, the floorboards had been pulled up, a hatchet lay at the doorway. The place was neat, clean, and empty. There was a small amount of food in the re-

147

frigerator, which was not connected to the electricity. Neither were the lights. The stove was an old-fashioned range and burned wood or coal.

"She . . . ," Helen began, and sobbed.

Jared put his arm about her shoulder. "We would have helped her," he said. "The hospital would."

"Is she dead?" asked Joel.

"I was informed only after she was taken to Indiana for burial," said the lawyer. "She had mailed me the will, and the title to this house. She had kept the taxes paid. She buried her brother and sister. She lived here alone."

"What am I supposed to do?" asked Jared.

"You look stranger all the time," Joel told him.

"Wouldn't you? Executor of a house stripped bare—I loved Taussig. She wouldn't let me help her."

"She didn't need help," said the attorney in a cold voice. "She left the hospital what will amount to a hundred thousand dollars."

There was a complete silence. Then Joel coughed. The lawyer glanced at him. "What will be done with that?" he asked.

Joel threw one hand outward. "I never knew the lady," he said. "Jared will think of something."

But Jared was still stunned. "Taussig . . . " He said gruffly. "She always showed good sense."

"She—the hospital was her life," said Helen, tears in her eyes.

"They would have taken care of her," Jared blurted. "She didn't . . . " His hands swept the dismal view of the empty house. "And what am I supposed to do?" He sounded angry.

"For now," said the lawyer, "accept the responsibility. The house will be sold. I can attend to that, if you and the hospital agree. Then we'll decide . . . "

"She wasn't crazy!" cried Jared.

"She had one wish. You can carry it out." Helen's hand lay on his shoulder.

"Do we have to do anything now?" asked Joel. "I'm a half-brother," he explained to the lawyer. "You've been in a bad spot, haven't you?"

"I hope I don't get another one like it," the lawyer assured him. "Here's my card. When Dr. O'Brien and the hospital have made some sort of plan, you can contact me."

Jared gave himself a shake. "I was shocked—" He apologized. "I thank you, sir. And I'll be in touch. Could we keep this out of the paper?"

"We have, so far. Except for the simple death notice."

"I feel sorry for him," said Helen when she joined the two doctors. "Jared, you are coming home with us?"

"I'm so damn busy, Mother. It's easier—"

"And lonelier."

"Yes. You're right. I'll come."

Helen smiled at Joel. "Thanks for the ride," she said. "Let's get along. Zenobia has a leg of lamb. And we'll help Jared on this Taussig thing—"

"If he asks me—"

"He seldom asks anything of anybody."

"No, he doesn't. That's damn selfish of him, isn't it?"

"It would be easier—"

"All right, you two," said Jared. "When you get me and my shortcomings fixed up, let's go eat dinner. I'll have to call in."

"So will I," said Joel. "Who gets the lady?"

"It's the lady's choice."

At the hospital there was boiling excitement about the hundred thousand dollars, what it would be used for. Every department had a perfect use for it. Several doctors could do some needed research. There was everything suggested from the purchase of some absolutely needed device to painting the walls of the cafeterias.

The newspapers had ideas just as comprehensive; letters were written to the editors. Joel began to collect these. "Hospital gowns—warmer floors in the rooms," he read. "Different colored uniforms for the different branches of the hospital. Paying the bills for people who were just beyond the edges of medicaid and other charitable sources. Something that would take the smell out of the hospital."

"Do we smell?" Joel asked innocently.

"We smell," Jared assured him. "I'm beginning to worry because the House smells funny to me."

"Oh, you're in a bad spot," Joel agreed solemnly. "A mixture of Zenobia's pot roast and the toilet water you brought Helen from England. That's bad . . . "

Jared lifted his head. "Are you writing these goofy letters?" he asked.

And Joel flared. As he did, generally, over unexpected things.

Jared assured him that he was destroying the image of the hospital.

"If anything that big doesn't have its image firmly established . . . "

"It used to have," said Jared coldly.

"And just what do you mean by that?" asked Joel coming close to him. Jared stood up. "No one but you would suggest different colors for different units. What if we overlap? There you'd be in purple, and you'd have to send a patient to Ortho, which would be in green. Or did you have yellow in mind?"

"I didn't have a damn thing in mind!" shouted Joel. "I read the damn letters from the *Post*."

"Someone wrote it."

And they were quarreling, hotly, loudly, when Brig came and told them that Joel's beeper and the telephone said that Joel was needed at the hospital. "Stat!" he added impressively.

Joel and Jared glared at each other, then laughed at Brig's use of the word. "I'll come with you," Jared offered.

"You've the wrong color coat," Joel told him. "It's Saturday night. I should stay there—in emergency—on Saturday nights." He went off mumbling about baseball, basketball—

"They are like five and ten," said Helen, watching them go along the drive and to their cars.

"They should be—and have been five and ten—" said Brig. "They are nice boys, Helen."

"Of course they are nice. And Joel should be mine."

"He thinks he is yours."

"Isn't it sad to look back on life's mistakes?"

"Could you have lived with the bishop for five years after he told you . . . ?"

"I could not. Not when I was twenty."

"Where are we going?" Jared had asked Joel. "And what do you expect?"

"Triage."

"To be brief."

"Yes."

"Some basketball game—"

"That's it. Two teams, two coaches, and the onlookers."

"Injuries?"

"Always."

"Why not call the police?"

"They are probably there, and maybe my team from

151

O.R." Joel had come out from the telephone, his face black with anger. "I'm not going into another high school locker-room fight," he told Jared.

"Don't you have to?"

"Have you ever been in one of those?" Joel demanded.

"No-o. Not really. I didn't play basketball."

"You could have played it, but not the way the kids today do it. I can't decide when they fight the worst. If they win or if they lose. And they certainly can send the wounded to City Hospital's E.R."

"Won't they do that on their own?"

"I don't think so. I have to make some delicate decisions. And inevitably I get into a fight of my own. I can't find anyone with sense to tell me what happened. The training of our students is involved. So me and my little black bag are supposed to handle twisted necks, broken jaws—and the language! You wouldn't believe the language!"

"What did you tell whoever called?"

"To get ambulances and take the injured to City."

"How many are hurt?"

"They didn't know."

"Good heavens!"

"They never heard of heaven."

"What are you going to do?"

"Stay right here until I get a call from my own hospital."

"Who called just now?"

"The police said things were getting out of hand. I suspect the ladies have got into the mess."

Jared began to take off his coat. Joel looked at him. "I thought—"

"I have that double renal transplant Monday morning, starts at three A.M."

"We'll get done by two."

"That's the sister giving her brother a kidney?"

152

"Yes."

"It's more worthwhile than this bunch of ruffians."

"One patient is like another," said Jared with exaggerated reproval. "And it sounds as if somebody was needed at the school."

"They have the police, which is what is needed."

"But, Joel—"

"Oh, shut up. Go on up to the House and eat dinner. What do you know about trauma?"

"I've studied medicine." Jared's voice and face were stiff. He went to Joel's car and opened the door. "Get in!" he said. "Hospital or high school?"

"I'm going to eat Zenobia's roast. You do the trauma."

Jared waited.

"You've no idea . . . ," said Joel, getting into the car seat.

"Then tonight you'll see that I do get an idea. Where did the police say for you to go?"

"To the school. And we should be telling the hospital—"

"Hadn't the hospital told *them* to call you?"

"Oh, get going, will you? There was something about a player's eye."

"And you've fooled around."

"I ordered an ophthamologist to be at the hospital."

"And all this time you've been fooling around." Jared started the car with a jerk.

"Better let me drive . . . ," said Joel, settling back into the car seat.

"Do you need your bag?"

"Not if we stay for any time at the school."

Jared stared at him. "Could you please tell the chauffeur which school . . . "

"I don't like sarcasm at a time like this."

"I don't like any part of this," said Jared. But he drove to the high school swiftly and safely. And he found just what

153

Joel had promised. A crowd of frightened, angry young people. Language to burn his ears. People pulled at him, pushed him.

He stood up on a chair. "Now you listen here!" he said loudly. "We're doctors, and we want all the people who are not bleeding out of this room in five minutes. We—"

"Ain't he pretty?" said a girl's high, clear voice.

Joel jumped to another chair. "If you want the people hurt to be cared for—"

The police were pushing the onlookers out, using some rough language of their own.

Both doctors were immediately and busily at work with swabs and bandages. The coaches assisted as best they could.

"There's a call for Dr. O'Brien," said someone at the door.

"Which O'Brien?" asked Joel, not lifting his head.

"You both—?"

"We both. Who called? Who's hurt? What happened?"

"It was the University Hospital, not City—"

"Get on the line," Joel told Jared. "They must have called the House."

"Trauma knows where you are."

"Go answer the phone."

Jared obeyed. "Put his arm in a sling of some kind," he called over his shoulder. And he did not return. Joel found himself stranded. "No dinner, no coat, no wheels," he complained.

The coach offered to drive him where he wanted to go. "What happened to the other man?" he asked Joel.

"I can call the hospital and find out," Joel offered.

"Would you do that? He wouldn't just go off and leave you?"

154

No. Jared would not. So Joel sought the telephone and dialed. The coach watched him. He was upset at the fight his "men" had got into. He would penalize—

"What happened?" he asked sharply, as Joel set the telephone down.

"Worse than a basketball fight. A man nearly got his scalp torn off."

"And your brother . . . ?"

"He can fix it if anyone can," said Joel. "I'm going to the hospital."

"Can I help?"

"You can watch. To see my brother do his microsurgery . . .

"Don't drive too fast," he told the coach, who was a very young man. "And don't talk. I haven't had my dinner. For that matter, Jared hasn't either."

"What will he do?"

"Put the scalp back. Tie together all the tiny blood vessels." He glanced at the coach. "He does it under a microscope with needles and sutures thinner than a human hair."

"And my guys were cussing out such a man?"

"He came with me. I do trauma. Injuries such as your team stirs up. Jared rode out with me and got called away."

"A scalp," murmured the coach. "Will it stay? I mean, and grow?"

"If the surgery goes well. Jared does all that kind of surgery." He reached for the telephone in the car. His own car did not have one. "I think I'll take up coaching," he said below his breath. He identified himself, got the hospital, said, "Mhmmmmmn. Mmnnnh. Yes, I'm coming in," and hung up.

"Man twenty," he told the coach. "Seventy percent of the scalp. Car accident."

"And your brother will reattach it?"

"Yes. He got a smart policeman who held the scalp in place."

"Your brother—"

"He and other microsurgeons have developed new surgical techniques. They have improved the successful reattachments of a hand, noses, ears, fingers—scalps—other facial skin. Parts of the foot—"

"There's the hospital," said the coach.

"I thank you for the ride." Joel was half out of the coach's car.

"You said—"

"If you can run fast enough." Joel was already a hundred feet toward the door.

But the coach was not allowed on the surgical floor. Joel thanked him, and got ready to change. Jared had left the keys to Joel's car at the desk. "But I'll stick around a while," he said. "Tell me, because old Jared will ask, did that girl's arm get splinted?"

"Who cares?" asked the coach angrily. "I'm getting a different job. I hate these fights."

"Maybe you could find a way to prevent them?"

The coach looked doubtful, and walked away. Joel went in to scrub. Sometimes Jared let him exchange instruments or something.

He was aware of Joel's presence. "How'd you get here?" he asked.

"Hooked a ride. Did you get anything to eat?"

"No. I'll have a break in about fifteen minutes. Get us both a sandwich."

Jared worked all night, but he was satisfied with the job. He would sleep for an hour or two, then pick up the tasks of

156

that day. Joel saw him briefly. "I had Ivory bring your car here," he said.

Jared smiled. Nodded. "Rub my neck, will you?" He was grey with fatigue. "Newspaper?" he asked.

"Of course. You're a hero."

"If the replant works."

"It always does."

They ate their breakfast in silence, and Jared took a shower, crawled into bed. Joel called the House, told Brig to watch the news and went across to his own job.

During the day, he checked on Jared, and on Jared's patient. At four o'clock, he told his brother to take a shower, get into clean clothes and come with him, out to the House and Helen and Brig.

"She'll want me to go to bed."

"Which you should do. But get away entirely for a couple of hours."

That was good therapy, and Jared went to his quarters. Joel spoke particulars to the dispatch desk.

He himself checked on the scalp patient, who was in intensive care, dead to the world. "Take good care of him," he said. "Dr. O'Brien needs a good meal and something besides a hospital to look at."

"He loves his work."

"I would not say 'love' just now," said Joel.

He wouldn't let Jared drive his own car. "I'll bring you back if you're needed."

"You'd argue."

"When did we ever argue?"

Jared laughed. "When didn't we?" he demanded. He stretched his long legs forward, laid his head back on the car seat, and, in five minutes, was asleep. Joel nodded, and greeted Helen with a finger to his lips. "He'll be awake very soon," he promised.

Helen told Brig that they should let the boys open the subject of what had happened the night before. Or was it two nights ago?

"The phone keeps ringing . . . "

"Let Joel handle it."

"Is he better at such things than Jared?"

"Jared satisfies himself by being the best microneurologist in the country. Personally I think he should get closer to people."

"Do you suppose this woman doctor who is coming . . .?"

"We don't need another doctor around here." Brig sounded angry.

"Well, a wife of any sort—"

"A bad wife is worse than a bad husband, my dear."

"How would you know?"

Brig laughed. "I've heard tell."

At dinner, it was Joel himself who brought up the fight in the high-school locker room. He concluded by saying he thought City Hospital should handle the injured at such contests.

"I understand," said Jared mildly, "that City emergency keeps pretty busy on Saturday nights. You could have sent one of your own residents out Saturday."

"They called me."

"Our hospital? Did they say you had to go?"

"I'm in charge of my own service," said Joel stiffly.

"And you like a fight."

Joel flared. "I do not like a fight! Not that kind. We maintain City Hospital to take care of such things."

Jared ate a forkful of salad. "And there was a bit of color,

158

too, mixed into the fight Saturday." There had been. And the language . . .

"I heard words," he said, "that I didn't know had been invented. Even when I was trying to help the guys, they—"

"I can deafen my ears to the language," said Joel. "But when I get man-handled . . . "

"And," Jared continued smoothly, "I was told that you had given orders that, in the future, we were not to accept calls from the city schools on Saturday night if the trouble was a fight."

"Why, you can't do that!" said Brig and Helen simultaneously.

"Why can't I?" Joel demanded, glaring at all three. Suppose Jared had got his operating arm broken Saturday night?"

"He didn't. And he was there of his own accord."

"And I did wrong to take him."

"You did wrong," said Jared, "to issue the order you did in our hospital emergency room. Fight or not, if we're needed, we are needed."

Joel leaned across the table. "Do you know what I think?" he demanded.

Jared shook his head. "I couldn't begin to imagine."

"Well, I think you belong in urology and not in emergency trauma. In other words, these calls are none of your business."

"And you did refuse to let the sainted surgeon of our hospital staff help out."

"I did refuse," said Joel firmly. "Last year I accepted such calls and had the injured brought to us. Their friends nearly wrecked the place when I ordered a man with a simple compound arm fracture to be sent to City Hospital.

159

They yelled and broke things. Scared the girls half to death. Those players are all big and strong, Jared, as you know, and smell like a rained-on skunk after a half hour of play."

"Joel, dear," Helen protested, but smiling.

"Well, they do, Helen. It wasn't the injured man who gave us trouble. It was the rest of the team. It seems their star player had a broken arm. My fault? Certainly not! Doesn't City have X-rays and splints? They do. We had a full trauma bay of our own that night. I sent this guy to City, and his friends began tearing up the place. I stopped them, and got called on the carpet the next day for 'allowing' it to happen. Hell, I didn't *allow* anything!"

"Joel, dear," said Jared, mimicking Helen.

"You know what happened," Joel pointed out. "You were on the review panel. At the time I thought you agreed that city games belonged to City Hospital."

"And you said then that you would refuse to go on such calls. Didn't you?"

"If I was busy. Saturday night our E.R. was comfortably busy, but I was out here, fixing to eat Zenobia's pot roast. I took you along to bolster my claim that City should attend to school fights. It's City Hospital's obligation."

"You were closer. And as a doctor, you are much better."

"Sure I'm better," said Joel. "But isn't it up to City to see that they have good doctors? And I'm going to tell the newspapers so."

Jared half rose from his chair. "Oh, no, you're not!" he said loudly.

"Then hadn't I better resign here?"

Jared sat down again. "No, you're not going to do that, either. So shut up on the subject."

Joel sat back, glowering. "I'm right," he growled.

"You're right. But you could be right, too, in saying that our med school here needs to raise the level of City's emergency care. Perhaps we should send out interns and residents to City for specified times to teach those chaps. Send them when the emergencies are thick or have them stay there long enough to teach younger doctors how to do whatever comes up."

"Have you told the chief that?"

"You do it."

"I won't."

And Joel was angry again. Brig stepped in. "Now you two stop it," he said sternly. "Three fights are three too many."

Joel stood up. "You're right," he said. "I'll clear out, now!"

"You can't do that," said Jared. "The Eckmans get here this Friday. I'll need you to help me."

Joel stared at him. "Lord help us," he said. "You have Helen and Brig, not to mention Zenobia and Ivory." He looked at Zenobia, then went to the pantry and leaned around the door post. "Helen," he called back, "do Zenobia and Ivory ever get a vacation?"

"Now would be the time . . .," said Jared, below his breath.

"Zenobia," Joel persisted. "You work around the clock, don't you?"

Zenobia's voice came calm, warm in reply. "I got me a good job here, Dr. Joel," she said comfortably. "And I don't cook dinner on Sunday."

"I know that. We get salmon salad."

Everyone laughed. "Yes," said Joel. "I know we do that. And you go to church. That's a big vacation!"

Zenobia came back into the room. "What would you-all do if I took one?"

"I can cook."

Jared snorted.

"Do you clean up after yourself?"

"Jared's the neat one."

Jared spread his very clean hands out on the table.
And everyone laughed.

"I'm right, though," Joel insisted.

"You are. They can go wherever and do whatever they
want. We'll pay for that." This from Brig.

"I'll tell you when, General," said Zenobia, going back
into the kitchen.

She returned with their dessert. "That young lady comin'
Friday?" she asked. "Do English girls . . ."

"She's a nice woman, Zenobia," Jared told her. "And her
father is coming with her."

"They don't do things that way these days, Dr. Jared."

"Well, these people do. And they'll eat and enjoy anything you cook."

"You thinkin' of marryin' her, Dr. Jared?" asked Ivory,
filling the port glasses.

In his own way each person at the table gasped. It had
been on each tongue, that question. But Zenobia was
shocked at her son. "Why you ask such a thing, boy?" she
demanded. "Don't you think it high time for Dr. Jared to
marry and have children?"

"It's been high time . . ." said Ivory.

"And he thinks we don't have troubles enough," laughed
Joel.

"Who cares what Ivory thinks?" asked Zenobia. "But tell
me one thing, Dr. Joel. Are you tired of my cooking?"

"Not me," said Joel hastily. "Not me!"

"He'd better not be," said Brig. "It's the best he'll ever
get for free."

Everyone laughed, and the family could hear Zenobia repeating the words to Ivory.

"But," said Brig, "since the matter has somewhat come up, tell us more about Miss—excuse me—*Doctor* Eckman, Jared. Are you, to coin an ancient phrase, sweet on the woman?"

Three heads turned sharply his way. Jared flushed, and as always, his hand went up to his cheek. "I've given it some thought."

"Will you tell us when you know?" asked Joel.

"Hush," said Helen. "We'll know."

Jared laughed. "Yes, you will, won't you?" He took the telephone from Ivory's hand. He got to his feet. "I'll take this out in the hall," he said. "It's from Los Angeles."

Helen held the phone, ready to hang it up. "He is listed in most large cities' telephone books," she said. "So patients can report to him if they want to."

"Usually it's a restored man's wife who has had a baby," Joel told them. "He's a great guy, Jared is. I hope this Eckman is the right kind."

9

The Eckmans arrived on Friday. Helen and Jared met their plane. Helen surveyed the strange English girl with approval. She was tall, with short, dark hair, and exquisite skin. She must be in her thirties. And Helen repressed a desire to ask why she had gone unmarried for so long. She contented herself by saying that Deborah did not look like a doctor.

"I shouldn't want to do that," said the young woman, and everyone laughed.

The visitors were enchanted with the House, the river, the well-kept grounds, Helen's flowerbeds. Zenobia and Ivory were properly introduced, and the guests were shown to their adjoining bedrooms on the second floor.

"I'll show you Jared's quarters," Helen promised, "sometime when he is not at home."

Deborah smiled. "You are of course very proud of him."

"He's been a good son. Yes, I am proud."

The enormous hospital astounded the visiting doctor. The wide, shining halls, the research laboratories. The discipline, the order. "Don't you get lost?" she asked Jared.

"Yes, I do. Often. But the people here are friendly and I am found again."

The microsurgeons and the ophthalmology staff ate lunch with her. "Would she demonstrate her technique?" she was asked.

"If a proper case comes in, and I have time to do it properly," she promised.

They were to stay five days.

The next day Joel offered to take them about the city. Brig said he would do it. "You're busy," he reminded the doctor.

"Yes, but—"

"Helen's sisters are coming for dinner."

"Can I weasel out?"

"I expect you to get a call."

Brig and Deborah's father got along famously. All things seemed to be going along famously. Deborah watched Jared operate; she heard him lecture to a class. She herself gave two lectures, using slides to show the surgery that she did.

"We could keep you here," the chief told her.

The hospital as a whole was fascinated. Had Dr. Jared finally found a girl?

They asked Joel. One bold man asked Jared.

Deborah herself asked Jared on the night that they walked along the river's edge at sunset.

"Isn't Lutie home?" Joel asked Helen.

"I don't know. Why?"

He hugged her. "You know why. May I follow them?"

"Jared and Deborah? Certainly not!"

"I want to see if he kisses her."

"Of course you do. I expect Deborah is curious, too."

She was. But Jared did not kiss her. And eventually Deborah asked him why. "Haven't you ever loved a woman?"

"Yes. Not since I had my jaw shot away."

"But the scar is not that bad."

"It's been bad enough. I am conscious of it when I am with a pretty woman."

"That is nonsense!"

Jared said nothing. He stooped and picked up a small stone, skipped it across the water.

"This afternoon," said Deborah, "I heard you talking to a woman who was refusing to have a needed mastectomy."

"Yes. She needs it. Her husband thought that his having a vasectomy would change her attitude."

"And you told him?"

"That I would do it only under protest."

"I heard you talking to her. I decided that you were well acquainted with women and their problems."

"I'm not." But he bent his head and swiftly kissed her cheek. She lifted her arms, pulled his head down, and kissed him.

At the top of the hill a shining, somewhat antiquated car rolled up to the front steps.

"My mother's older sisters," said Jared. "We invite them for six, they arrive at four. Brig and your father have not returned from the ball game."

"I wonder what my father made of it," said Deborah, and laughed.

"He's a well-read man. He knew it couldn't be cricket." They walked along, and went into the house through the kitchen. Zenobia made pointing gestures to the living room.

"We saw them," said Jared. "Can you drop a pan or some such thing so we can get up the back stairs?"

Zenobia giggled. But the men's arrival covered their flight upstairs to dress for dinner. "Give yourself an hour," Jared told Deborah.

"I—"

"I know. So can I. But if you take that hour you won't be sorry."

The aunts could be heard talking. Charlotte was getting a little deaf and thought everyone else was. Jared and Deborah hurried upstairs. And met Joel coming down. He pointed to the lower rooms.

"We know," said Jared. "We're escaping for an hour."

"Make it a solid one," Joel advised. "Aunt Charlotte is primed. And Aunt Adelaide has new eyeglasses. She's ready to consult Debbie."

"Don't let him make you laugh," Jared warned. "They'd be upstairs with us. Remember my mother was a younger member of the family, and not very bright."

"Why, Doctor . . ."

Jared winked at her, and Joel took her arm, led her to her bedroom door, put her inside, and firmly closed her in. "I gave her an hour," said Jared.

"Good. You go take the same. And don't wear a white coat, you get the sleeves too smudged."

Jared nodded. "I remember the last dinner party," he confessed. "What do they think I do at the hospital?"

Joel closed the door on him. And Jared prepared to take a hot bath.

He came down exactly an hour later, dressed in a crisp blue and white seersucker suit, worn with a dark blue turtleneck shirt. Joel put his finger beside his nose. They would soon find out what the aunties would say about that outfit. He was wearing a linen jacket over a white shirt and brown tie. Dark trousers.

They stood in the doorway. "You look like a clothing-store salesman," Jared told Joel.

"Listen," said Joel.

Deborah was saying, in her clear, crisp British voice, the

167

thing that really intrigued her at the hospital was the estab-
lishment of I.V. teams to institute venal feedings. "Our
medics waste so much time finding veins," she was saying.

Joel's elbow pushed into Jared's side and he said,
"Ouch!"

So loudly that everyone turned to look at him.

"You dope," said Joel, going over to Deborah and kissing
her. "You're lovely," he said. As indeed she was in a long
skirt of various pink plaids and a lace-trimmed blouse of
darker pink.

The older men came downstairs, talking about the ball
game. "You should have gone with us," Mr. Eckman told
Deborah. He was a very tall, slender man, with a reserved
face and manner.

"He'll tell you all about it," said Brig wickedly.

"How is the visit going?" Aunt Adelaide asked.

"Jared, aren't you going to dress for dinner?" Aunt Charlotte asked simultaneously.

Which made everyone laugh. Jared went across the
room and put his arm in a sheltering gesture about his
mother's shoulders.

"How *is* it going?" he asked softly.

"About as usual."

"Be careful."

"I shall. Here comes Ivory. You might help him, dear."

"Joel's braver."

"You do it."

So Jared did go to the obviously nervous houseman. He
took two delicate wine glasses and approached Deborah,
who had been cornered by Aunt Charlotte. Deborah took
one glass, Aunt Charlotte did not. "You know my habits,
Jared," she said sternly.

"Yes, I do," Jared told her, lifting the glass to his own
lips.

"Is this American wine?" asked Deborah innocently.

Aunt Adelaide was just as firmly refusing the glass offered to her by Ivory.

Joel took it, and joined Deborah and Jared. "We've heard the lecture," he told the young woman.

Helen's dinner table was lovely. A stretch of satiny Irish linen with crystal in a thistle pattern to match the cloth and gleaming silver; single white blossoms floated in small glass bowls. Brig took Deborah to his end of the table; Jared was to sit at her other side. Helen was escorted by Mr. Eckman, with Joel beside her. The aunts sat facing each other.

"Are you going to stay here very long?" Aunt Charlotte asked Deborah.

"We are traveling to other cities in the States," said Deborah. "I am interested in various medical techniques."

"But especially Jared's, I understand."

"Yes, because I do microsurgery myself. I am not so diversely skillful as he is."

"I don't like to talk about operations and such things at the table," said Aunt Adelaide. "But if you are a doctor in England, I suppose you work without pay. I know people who are sick there don't pay."

Deborah glanced at her father. "He is in government," she explained. "We have National Health Service, paid for through taxes. Yes. I do some work for that service. But I am especially in private health service, which Jared tells me works as yours does. Insurance and privately paid accounts. There actually is no competition between NHS and private practice. Eventually the government hopes to use private health service as a bridgehead so that the National Health Servie will be insurance-based rather than dependent on general taxation. A person who needs eye service cannot wait three or four years to be attended to. And I agree with the lady who does not like to talk about medical matters at table."

"Does the government now give your private medical people a free road?" asked Brig.

"So long as it is not a Labor government," said Deborah. "At present we do not have that."

"If you marry Jared, you'd come over here and you would be free to do as you choose."

"That's a big 'if,' Aunt Charlotte," said Joel.

"I shouldn't think so. I saw her kissing him this afternoon."

Jared opened his mouth to speak, as did Deborah. Jared won the race. "Aunt Charlotte," he said smoothly, "did you marry every man you kissed? When you were young?"

"Yes," said Joel silkily. "I think she did."

There was laughter, suppressed at first, then rising in volume.

"I should send you from the table," Helen told Joel. "I think we had better stick to medical talk."

"I wouldn't have a female doctor," said Aunt Charlotte crisply.

"I hope you won't ever need one," said Deborah, gently. "You were asking me, General," she said to Brig, "if a private health doctor in England made a good living."

"That was rude of him," murmured Helen.

"It was a purely political discussion," Brig insisted. "And she took it as such. She said she made the equivalent of seventy-five thousand dollars last year."

"I am highly specialized," said Deborah. "But I think general practitioners make a proper living if they are at all good. Mrs. Morse, what is this delicious fowl we are eating?"

Helen laughed a little, knowing that the subject was not

170

necessarily being changed. "It's capon, dear," she said gently. "Zenobia makes almost anything delicious."

But Aunt Charlotte would not be diverted. "What happened to the girl who used to live next door?" she asked Jared.

"She still lives there," said Jared smoothly.

"I thought she married when you got shot up in Vietnam."

"She did," said Jared, still smoothly. "Brig, will you have Ivory bring Deborah some more capon? And we'll let Joel tell his only joke."

"Neither you, nor Joel," said Helen firmly, "is too old to be sent from the table."

This caused laughter, and finally, a discussion of what a sacrifice was, and why. This was covered and everything else concerning the ball game, from uniforms to ball boys. All of which got pretty hilarious.

The aunties always went home early, and this evening Helen delegated Joel to drive behind their car and see them safely into their home.

"Why me?" he asked. "Didn't you hear Aunt Adelaide explain that I was no relative?"

"I did. Perhaps Jared and Deborah would like to ride with you?"

"Deborah, yes. That guy in the turtleneck shirt, no deal."

But Jared did go, and afterward the three enjoyed a drive through the suburbs.

"If I had let Jared and Deborah go together," Joel told Helen the next day, "we'd be having a wedding."

"Why not?"

"You know why not. The guy's never got over Lutie."

That same next day they all went to church, and Jared

read the lessons. That afternoon they had various callers from the medical field. Monday morning Helen and Brig drove their guests to their plane. Yes, they would return, if Jared should get an eye case before they returned to England. . . . And they hoped that might happen.

The night before Joel had asked Jared, "This afternoon, did you ask Deborah to marry you?"

"No," said Jared.

There was a pause of several minutes. Then, "She asked me not to," said Jared.

He could hear Joel jump on the bed springs. "I would . . ." he began.

"Yes. She and I both knew that you would."

Joel sighed heavily. "She is a lovely woman."

"Go to sleep," said Jared. "The trauma chief has to meet the press as of tomorow morning."

Joel sighed again. "I always say all the wrong things."

"They expect you to. And the women needle you."

"They yell so to get attention," Joel explained. "Reporters."

The next afternoon he came to the House before Jared did and sat on the porch with Helen. They discussed the Eckmans. Brig liked them because he could understand the Englishman when he talked, said Helen.

Joel nodded. "Wasn't she lovely, Helen?" he asked dreamily.

"Deborah? Yes, she was lovely."

"Her skin was like rich, expensive silk, the lovely line of her cheek and jaw, the way her eyes are set . . . " He shifted and looked up at Helen.

She patted his shoulder. "I am sure you know what to do," she said.

"If old Jared . . . "

"Old Jared had—has—the same chances that you do, my dear.

"You've been so good to me."

"You owe us nothing, my son."

But within twenty-four hours things seemed to have changed.

The morning's news conference had had time to be reported on the radio, and printed in the evening newspaper.

"I told them I would say all the wrong things," said Joel. "Can't we talk of other things, Helen?"

"I can. What's on your mind?"

"Why do you suppose Deborah told old Jared not to ask her to marry him?"

"Because she felt sure she was going to say yes."

"And she didn't want to?"

"Does Jared know that?"

"You are aware as much as I am of what Jared knows."

Joel sighed and went to the phone to answer his beeper. He returned to say that he would have to go back to the hospital. "It's been a day," he told Helen. "A news conference, and now trouble in the emergency room."

"What sort of trouble?"

"Maybe I'll tell you when I get home."

"Jared must still be at the hospital?"

"Jared doesn't even know where the emergency room is, sweetheart."

He kissed her, and ran out to his car, going around the drive much too fast.

A fight. A fight in E.R. That could mean anything.

He reached the interstate and obeyed the rules, his mind on a dozen things. The truck that passed and almost clipped him. That would have made a nice accident, whizzed him around in front of the cars on the westbound

173

lane. There was a pretty scene, a pasture with sheep on its green grass. That close to the city? Deborah. Would she ever live in this country? He had touched her. He had danced with her. He could not cut in before Jared got moving. For such a handsome, such a very smart guy, old Jared did strange things. Like not wanting to marry the woman he loved because he had a hole in his cheek.

He thought of the basketball game a week ago. Jared had jumped in ready to help him and tell him to shut up. Not to say that the city's public schools should call only on City Hospital's E.R. Well, as usual he'd probably been right. That Joel popped off too much.

But that morning, Joel had said the same things again. And to the news reporters. The matter of color had come up as well as the fighting, but he thought it had been handled. University Hospital made no color distinctions. They just ran their own system, and charged for care. But in the case of inability to pay, they did a lot of charity work. It would just be neater, more reasonable, for the University Medical School to train men to handle the sort of cases that came into City's E.R. The newspaper account of the conference had repeated remarks on the roughhousing and Joel's hot answers. Well—no more news conferences. No matter what the chief said.

He had *not* said that the big, handsome—and private—University Hospital was too good to take care of high-school game roughhousers. He had just said that the tax-supported hospital should take care of the city tax-supported schools' problems. He, like any doctor, would answer any call, but no doctor could be everywhere.

The sun lowering in the sky shone handsomely on University Hospital's red brick and white granite buildings. Lord, the place was big!

The parking lot for the trauma bay and E.R. was unusually crowded for a late Monday afternoon. Cars, and people. Someone yelled at him, and he lifted his hand—he was a friendly guy—and decided to go down into the basement garage where he had a space. Some of the crowd up here looked rough. He touched the button and the door lifted.

"Hurry up, Doc," the attendant called to him.

Joel hurried.

"What goes on?" he asked, slipping out of the seat.

"Fight in E.R. Somebody got hurt, I guess."

Why should there be a fight in E.R.? Joel began to run. As he stepped out of the elevator he began to pull free of his jacket, one he was fond of. He had had it made in Hong Kong and had worn it that morning for the lecture.

"Hey!" he cried, for someone, coming up behind him, had got him caught with his arms half out, half in, the sleeves. Someone's foot tripped him and he crashed to the floor.

"I'm the doctor," he tried to say and felt a rubber shoe sole strike his mouth.

There was a fight, all right. Well, he could fight, too. Only—he could not. Not a dozen tall boys. They kicked him. He rolled, and did his best—and passed out.

He was being beaten. He became conscious again. He saw a woman coming toward him. A woman? She had a stick of some sort. It slashed across his forehead. He tried to roll over the other way to protect his face. Where was good—old—Jared?

Good old Jared was standing at the foot of his bed. His bed? Why—and he drifted off—came back—and began to struggle. "Hold it!" said Jared's firm voice.

He "held it" because he hurt. There were sounds. Was

he in O.R., and hurting this way? His mask had slipped down over his eyes. "Wipe," he said faintly.

"Shut up," said Jared's voice.

"Wh . . . ?"

"You're in bed, and you hurt. And you're to lie still!" said Jared's voice again.

Joel tried to say "Preacher," found that he could not, so he went to sleep again.

The evening before, Jared had been eating dinner—Zenobia's delicious crab salad—when the call came from the hospital. His secretary said he had better come, sir. "Your brother's been hurt. We had a riot here in trauma E.R. . . ."

Jared waited for no more. He briefly repeated what Tucker had said.

"He was beeped," said Helen, rising in agitation.

Jared touched her shoulder. "I'll call back," he said. "If he was hurt, you couldn't help."

And he was gone.

When he returned home he told Helen and Brig that Joel was indeed badly hurt. "So far as I could make out the whole basketball team laid for him in trauma E.R. and beat him up."

"Why?" asked Helen, rising from her chair.

Jared gently pushed her down. "You can't go to him, dear," he said firmly. "He's in intensive care. I was allowed in only because I was a doctor. And his brother."

"But why was he attacked?" Tears were running down Helen's cheeks. Jared went to her, and with a doctor's touch used his handkerchief to brush them away.

"He talked too much," said Jared. "Remember? We were called out a week ago—he was—because of a fight and injuries at a basketball game in one of the north city schools. Joel said that University Hospital should not be

176

called for such things, and he said it again in a speech he made yesterday morning. He said that City Hospital should care for the city schools and their medical problems."

"Shouldn't they?" asked Brig, who was looking angry.

"If equipped and staffed. Evidently Joel's remarks came out to say that University was too good to attend the basketball players. Anyway, they ganged him."

"Is he hurt so badly, Jared?"

"He's hurt. Something about his head, they fear for his eyes. His head is wrapped up big as a basket of washing, so I couldn't tell. One arm has a cast, and I think he was kicked—anyway hurt—in the groin. These characters use that means on a fellow. And it does hurt."

"You're going back . . ."

"I'm going to stay at the hospital. Yes."

"I'll bet he makes a terrible patient," growled Brig.

"He will. He does," Jared agreed. "That's why I am going to stay with him. But, Brig, you might—"

"I'll do what I can," Brig agreed. "He had a right to say what he did."

Of course there was an uproar. The newspapers, the local radio, TV and pictures. Even the bishop was mentioned, and a long article published about *him*. How had that come up? One of the aunties had talked, suggested Helen. Charlotte was no relation to Joel. She was busily reading the list of his injuries. A broken wrist bone. Possible internal injuries from being pummeled and kicked. Cuts on his face. It was too soon to determine if his eyes were hurt.

Deborah called from California, and sounded almost hysterical. Was she needed?

They knew very little about the face injuries. But she

177

was more than welcome to come. Yes, his eyes could have been hurt. Jared had seen his face unwrapped. There was an angry, bloody scar above the eyes from temple to temple.

"A knife?"

"He talks about an umbrella rib."

He also said that a girl had done that. Which seemed absurd. But was not. Deborah said she would come.

Brig said he would talk to the school board, to the police. He was the "boy's" stepfather. And the Brigadier General, Retired, made a good impression.

But when Deborah arrived, Joel was still heavily sedated.

And when he aroused somewhat he was very depressed. Even after she came— "If my eyes are gone," he growled, "don't think anyone should bother."

Jared heard him and said that he needed another kick.

Joel did not respond.

"I thought he'd ask me where I'd find a place," Jared told the women. "It's not like Joel—"

No, it was not like the usually laughing, joking man. "Me and my big mouth," he kept saying.

"You said just the right things," Jared told him. "We are going to send trauma residents to City Hospital on critical nights."

Deborah sat by the bed and held his hand. He showed no response. "If I'm blind . . .," he would say, and stop.

"We haven't really examined your eyes."

"That girl—"

"What girl?"

But he wouldn't say. He'd just get into more trouble. The girl had attacked him; she had had—he *knew* it was a spoke from an umbrella! But—he turned his head away,

178

and Helen and Deborah could not talk him out of his "low." This often happened after severe traumatic injury. Joel had told them that. "I know what happened. I go through it ten times a night."

Deborah said she meant to examine his eyes, ready to operate. Jared agreed it should be done.

And Lutie's father chose that critical time to die.

Jared received the news, white-faced, dumb. He wanted to go to Lutie. He had his own work stacked at the hospital. He was the only one who could get any response from Joel. Lutie wanted him to conduct the funeral— "But I can't ask him," she said. Poor girl, the death had come suddenly, unexpectedly. Helen tried to comfort her, knowing that Jared could have done so. He shook his head when the funeral was mentioned. "I'll assist, if I have time," was all he would say to Helen.

Of course he went to see Lutie, and tried to comfort her, holding her tight in his strong arms. "You and Maggie come up to our house," he told her.

"I'm all right. You attend to Joel. Have you told him?"

"Not yet."

"I'll do it."

"No, you won't. I'm busy up above my head. I don't want you in the same fix."

She wanted to ask if Deborah was planning to stay. Jared knew that she did. He told his mother to tell Lutie that they were hoping Deborah could do something about Joel's eyes.

"She knows she's a doctor, dear."

"And that she's a woman."

"You feel that she is jealous?"

"Yes," said Jared, and he walked away.

Lutie told Brig and Helen that she planned to sell the

179

farm. "If you know of anyone who would make a good neighbor . . ."

Helen looked at Brig. "You and Jared would," he said bluntly.

"But Jared wants Deborah . . ."

When Deborah had arrived, Brig had met her and taken her to the house. As best he could, he told her what had happened. "You were still here when he made his talk about City Hospital emergency room attending accidents at the city schools."

"What he said seemed reasonable to me."

"These characters—the pupils at this particular school—seem to have been hunting for a reason to bring up a fight. So far as Joel said, color was not an issue. It was simply a matter of how much work, and what work, the two hospitals could do."

"Have you seen him?"

"He's in intensive care. Helen has seen him, and Jared spends every spare minute with him. In his silent, odd way he blames himself somewhat."

"How could he? I think I heard him tell Joel not to talk—*sound off* was the term he used."

"They argued about it, yes."

"I must see Lutie if possible."

"I think Jared expects me to bring you directly to the hospital. We are all being very busy—"

"I am sure you are. But Joel must understand . . ."

"He's in the dumps. I've never seen him give up before."

"Oh, dear," said Deborah. They had reached the hospital. Jared came out and kissed her, in front of a dozen personnel.

"As if things weren't complicated enough," Brig reported to Helen.

They were indeed complicated, and everyone was very busy. Jared did assist with the funeral. Deborah watched him closely. Why had he not gone into the church? He presided so beautifully. Calm. Assured. His vestments suited his tall, well-carried person.

But medicine would have known a great loss. And she realized that his father's behavior had influenced his attitude toward the church.

"I think," she told Helen, "that he was very noble to do anything at all in the church."

Helen turned to look at the tall young woman, trim, lovely, in her brown linen suit. "He thought first of the church as such, and what it meant to me."

"It continues to do so?" Deborah asked curiously.

"One man could not destroy the church," said Helen gravely.

"Does Joel feel as you do?"

"I have never talked to Joel about his feelings toward the church. He sometimes attends service. He helps Jared."

And she told of the old nurse who had died. "Joel talks all the time, but says very little under certain circumstances. He knew the bishop, his father, and he fights down his hatred of him."

"As you do?"

"Mine was hurt. Not hatred."

After the funeral, that same afternoon, Jared came for Deborah, and took her to see Joel. Joel was aware of who she was, and held her hand. "Will you . . .?" he asked.

"I'll stay until we've examined your eyes." She sat down beside his bed. "You go on," she told Jared.

She sensed Joel's depression. She studied his charts. She talked to the staff eye man. They thought the cornea of one eye could be saved. He was badly hurt.

"He said a girl slashed him with the metal spoke of an umbrella. She must have had such an injury in mind."

"These young hoodlums— I was told by witnesses that Joel was totally unprepared."

"When can we look at his eyes?"

"Tomorrow. If you're ready."

"I don't know that I can help."

"He thinks you may. And that's a big step already taken. Do you have your instruments?"

"Yes, I've been doing demonstrations. Besides, Dr. O'Brien—"

"Jared you mean? Yes, he'd have what you need. And he'd assist if you do operate."

"We'll see."

Lutie had stood up well through her father's funeral. But Helen went with her to the house, to suggest, she said, that the young woman come up to the House, to see Maggie, and perhaps spend the night."

"Isn't Deborah there?"

"We have two guest rooms."

Lutie knew that. She knew, and loved, the House as much as Jared did. She would stay in her own home, was her reply. "I wish Joel were not hurt, and in the hospital."

Zenobia had been taking care of the little girl. "Spoiling her rotten," said Brig.

Zenobia acknowledged that she had done so, with Brig's help. "Who brought her that basket of twin dolls with all the cloes an' fixin's?" she asked.

But eventually Lutie did agree to spend the night. "Where is Jared?" she asked.

"He said he had a heavy surgery schedule. A kidney

transplant became available. He never really talks to me about his work."

"I know. Is Dr. Eckman at the hospital?"

"Yes. Joel clings to her. I suppose he believes she can save his eyes."

"I cannot think of Joel blind," said Lutie sadly.

"Joel can't, either. He is frightened by the thought."

"I can't imagine him frightened, either."

"You like him, don't you, Lutie?"

"Of course I like him. I would suppose that everyone would like Joel."

"Jared . . . ," said Jared's mother.

"He's quiet. He keeps his feelings swallowed within himself. I think that when he knew how badly he was hurt in Vietnam he made a real decision. Either be passive and live on drugs until he died. Or find some way to work, keep busy. You were probably what made him decide—"

"And you."

"No. Before then he had told me that he could never marry me. I supposed there was some other woman. I was hurt, and frightened, and I married George Reeves. I knew that I had done the wrong thing the first night. Oh, Helen—"

Helen comforted her. "You made him a good wife. Jared thinks so. He knows he was to blame."

"And now. . . . Will he marry Deborah?"

"Oh, no!" said Helen quickly. "He brought her to America because of the surgery she does. We have to face the fact that Jared is a surgeon first, and a man second. Anyway, she's sure to marry Joel."

Lutie looked up in surprise.

"If she marries anyone," Helen amended her statement.

"Does Joel know this?"

"He may. Before Deborah left for California, he told me that he loved her."

"Does Jared know all this?" Lutie sat staring into the fire, her head turned away from Helen.

Struck by Helen's silence, she looked up. Lutie had beautiful, expressive eyes. "Will someone tell him?" she asked. Her hands twisted together in the lap of her dark green skirt.

Helen sighed. "I suppose someone will," she said softly. "And he could love her and marry her. But he loves you the most, Lutie."

Lutie said nothing. But her eyelashes were wet upon her cheek.

10

The next day, Joel's eyes were to be examined, and it was hoped that Deborah could do her delicate surgery upon both of them, though she feared that one was not a hopeful thing. It was a delicate procedure. Jared had thought he would be present, then decided that he would not go into the operating room. His feelings were too strong. He could trust Deborah. Joel would ask for him if he wanted him.

He had his own schedule of patient interviews, but no surgery. Knowing what was happening over in the ophthalmalogical building he could feel tension mounting within him. All doctors, all surgeons, he thought, knew this tension. It was why he had decided not to observe Deborah work upon Joel.

"I didn't know how much I loved the guy," he thought. The words seemed to be imprinted on his brain.

And when the phone rang, when Tucker answered, he could feel the chill on his arms, the stiffness in his neck.

"Dr. Eckman wants you to come to assist her," said the secretary quietly.

Jared stood up. "I have a schedule . . ."

185

"You seem to be needed, Doctor," said Tucker, who was an enviably quiet person.

"Needed how?"

"They didn't say. Just that you were needed in ophthalmology surgical, *stat!*"

Jared stood up. "I'll go," he agreed. He should have been there all along.

He went out into the hall. The hospital was too big. There were rules against running. And unwritten ones, he thought, against a surgeon being afraid. It was not the first tension he had ever felt before surgery. He could and would talk it down. But his own brother . . .

Things were normal in the corridors, in the elevators. "Calm yourself," he ordered his mind, his hands, his nerves. "She just wants you to see something. You want this to go well. Concentrate and do whatever Deb wants you to do. Probably only to talk to Joel, who can be fractious . . ."

But he could not separate himself from the fact that this was his brother who waited in the O.R. That Deb had, or would, know what to do. That she had the skill, equal to his own . . .

Tucker was walking with him. Why? Had Jared asked him to? Jared looked at the man. "Go back and get my surgical kit," he said.

"Doctor . . ."

"I don't know what they want me to do. Maybe only to see what they have done . . ."

Tucker turned and went along the hall. Jared rubbed his hands together. Things would be all right. Joel, like most trauma patients, was overreacting. Deborah thinks I can quiet him down. Traumas are always difficult to deal with.

186

He should have thought of that. One could not expect a trauma hurt as Joel had been to listen to instructions and cooperate. I should not have left Deb on her own. She wasn't, really. The whole damn staff were available.

He reached O.R. A nurse was holding a green gown for him. Jared wanted to ask her what was up, but restrained himself. He went in and scrubbed, talking silently to himself. Deb came out, her eyes big.

"Trouble?" Jared asked her.

"With me, yes. I can't operate on Joel. Could you . . . ?" There were a dozen or more microsurgeons in that hospital.

"I'll see," said Jared, letting the nurse fold the towel over his hands.

Cap, mask—he was walking to the table where Joel lay covered by a sheet. What sort of anesthesia, he asked, reading the vital signs as he spoke.

Local. All right. He could talk to Joel. And to himself. "You are not afraid. Just another patient." He studied Deb's eyes. "You won't need to stay," he said.

But she had received the roll of instruments. Tucker must have run all the way, and cut a dozen corners. Jared checked.

"Did you bring your scissors?" asked Joel from the head of the table.

Jared jumped, but he made himself laugh. For his own sake. The cornea of an eye was a delicate bit of material with which to work. He had watched Deb do what she now found herself unable to do. He held out his gloved hand and felt the tension drop. Rowena, his own chief nurse, had made that run with Tucker. "You must have used roller skates," he said, testing the rigidity of Joel's head. He bent

187

over, opened his palm for the first instrument. "Then give me a sponge on a stick," he said. Rowena, of course, had one ready. And he went to work.

She never got tense. Or did she? "How you doin'?" Jared asked her.

"Forgetting who this is," she said. She understood. Deb came back into the area. She began to talk quietly to Joel— and Jared worked. One eye, the other—

He himself bandaged them, he bandaged the head. "Take him to recovery," he said, "but no sedation. I'll need him to know what is happening. Deb, you'll stay with him?"

She looked up in surprise. "Of course, Doctor. And thank you. I—" But Jared was gone.

"He has other patients," said Rowena, gathering the instruments, which she would take back through the halls, sterilize, and have ready—

That evening, when he told the family about the matter, he mentioned his fear, his tremor. "I had no business touching my brother," he said firmly. "Whether one knows it or not, acknowledges it, the love is there, and the thought that I might injure him—"

"You couldn't," said Helen firmly.

"You don't know microsurgery, my dear," said her son.

"I suppose Joel is in intensive care?"

"Recovery. And we won't know for some days if the surgery was a success."

"The newspapers say it was," said Brig.

Jared swore a little. "How those reporters can sniff a story—"

"It's their business, dear," said Helen. "Just as it was yours to try the surgery, the only hope of saving Joel's eyes."

188

"It had to be done. We couldn't let him be blind." And again he felt the tremor.

"If—" She stopped and did not speak further until Jared urged her to say what she had meant to say. "If Deborah loves Joel," she said slowly, "wouldn't she have been nervous, too?"

Jared rose, went over and kissed his mother's cheek. "You are a very smart woman," he told her.

"Has it taken you thirty-seven years to find that out?" asked Brig gruffly.

"Only to acknowledge it," said Jared.

Throughout the house, the atmosphere lightened. Lutie decided to return to her own home. "I have a thousand things to do," she said.

"Jared will help you," said Helen, picking up her needlepoint. "Unless he is going back to the hospital."

"I am," said Jared. "But later."

So he helped gather things that Maggie's short visit had scattered about the house. He carried sleepy Maggie out to the car, and after the child was tucked into bed, he helped Lutie decide what she would do with her father's clothing. "Let it wait a day or two," said Jared.

"It only gets harder," said Lutie. "His personal things, his watch and books—those I'll keep. I'll hate to sell the farm, Jared."

"Don't make any decision on that, either, for a time. If I leave now, will you go to bed and sleep?"

"I will, if you go home, wash your face, and put on some clean clothes."

He stared at her. "Did I get smudged?"

"You did, and while it is becoming, the personnel at the hospital may not think so."

Jared bent and kissed her cheek. "You're smudged, too," he told her. And went out the door, leaving her to stand

189

watching him get into the car, drive up the hill, and go into his own home.

"Do you have to go back to the hospital?" Helen asked him. "Deborah phoned and said Joel was in a stable condition, whatever that means."

"I felt that I should have stayed with Lutie. Her father's death hasn't hit her yet."

"She'll handle it."

Jared nodded, and went upstairs to "wash his face and change his shirt." He repeated the words as he walked about his room. "She sounded so—so domestic," he told himself. If only, he thought—

He went to the hospital, made bedcheck, looked through some mail, and found that Joel was indeed in good condition. He drove Deborah home. "I can't thank you enough," he told her.

"There is time ahead."

"You're tired."

"Aren't you?"

"Yes. Now that you mention it. Yes. I am. Do you want to drive Joel's car? If not, Brig stands ready to chauffeur you about."

So things would settle down into what he again recognized as domesticity. And it was a good feeling.

Joel progressed rapidly. "He's as strong as a bull," said Brig.

"And as stubborn," Jared agreed.

Joel's abdominal injuries had about healed. His arm would. Now, if when the time came his eyes—

"That girl really gave him a lick," Jared told the family. He had said the same things a dozen times before.

"Have they identified her?" asked Deborah.

"Yes. And they have her in restraint. And we are waiting to see if Joel will want to file any charges—"

190

"He won't," said Helen quietly. "He'll see that she is sent to some sort of corrective home. But—dreadful things like 'charges.' No, that's not Joel."

Deborah smiled and nodded. "I would have said not," she agreed.

The next day Dr. Eckman took the outer bandages from Joel's eyes. "Where's old Jared?" he asked. "I don't see him anywhere."

"He's in surgery," said Deborah. "I am your doctor."

"How am I?"

"Your condition is satisfactory."

"Can't you take the patches off?"

"Not yet. Be quiet."

Joel grumbled but lay still. When he was being moved into his room, he asked that Jared be told to come to see him.

"Wait until late afternoon," said Deb when she caught up with Jared. "He expected us to take off the patches this morning. He needs rest."

Even during that first night, Joel asked for Jared.

"He was here, but he went home," the head nurse told him. "The man works too hard, and you had to give him some more things to worry about."

"Send him in first thing in the morning," said Joel.

The nurse made no reply. She knew that Dr. Jared would be at the hospital early, and would hurry to the surgical building first thing. She herself would be off duty.

"You may as well go to sleep now," she told her patient.

"How can you tell if I'm awake or asleep, all these patches and bandages?" grumbled Joel, his voice softening. And drifting away. The nurse watched him. "He doesn't know it, but he's asleep," she told herself.

But by morning he was wide awake. He wanted to get up and go to the bathroom. He could feel his way.

"Are you allowed out of bed?" asked the nurse.

"PRN," said her patient.

"Well, PRN says 'no,' you lie still. I'll bring you whatever you need. I have my orders, you know."

"We can chain him down," said Jared's voice behind her.

She jumped. "He doesn't know much about being sick," she told the tall man in white.

"I'll handle him," Jared promised. "You can take a break. Has he had breakfast?"

"The orders say he can't have anything but juice."

"Then get him some juice. What do you want, Joel?"

He would not answer. "I can't even shake my head," he complained.

"And why do you suppose that is?" asked Jared, picking up the chart. "You slept all right."

"That's what you think," Joel retorted. "When will they know about my eyes?"

"And you wanted to go into the bathroom to peek under the bandages," said Jared. "I know your type."

Joel made a growling sound, then his lips curved into a smile. When Jared lifted his wrist to count his pulse, Joel clung to his hand. "I made a fool of myself," he said gruffly.

"You got into a mess the same as I did," Jared told him. "We both went where we had no business being. Quiet down now."

"I can't go home?"

"Not for a time, Buddy. Deborah is your doctor, not me."

"You know?" said Joel, plucking at the gauze that wrapped his face. "I just may marry Deb."

Jared laughed shortly. "If she'll have you."

"She will. And you'll marry Lutie."

192

"Who arranged all that?"

"We did. Before I was hurt. Deb and I'll buy and live in Lutie's house. You'll marry Lutie. And together we'll build a small house for Brig and Helen."

"Do Lutie and Brig and Helen know about all this?"

"We'll tell 'em."

The nurse returned, and with her Dr. Eckman and the cart. "We're going to remove the heavy outer bandages," she told Joel, after the preliminaries of chart reading and all were over. "Jared is staying."

Joel clung to her hand. "Let her work," said Jared softly. "She's the doctor for now, Joel. You lie still and let her do what she must."

Joel straightened in the bed, and Deborah cut away the heavy wrappings, leaving only the patches and a thin gauze wrap over his eyes.

"Can you tell?" Joel asked her, urgently.

"Can you see light," she asked him in turn.

"Not with the patches on."

"And they must stay on for a time, my friend. I hope I can trust you, Joel."

"You can't," said Jared. "When I got here this morning he was ready to get out of bed and go look in the bathroom mirror."

"Joel?" asked Deborah.

"He didn't let me," said Joel meekly.

He made a restless patient. Helen came to sit with him, and Lutie. And, when he could, Jared did. Deborah was in and out. And Joel asked her for Jared.

"Doesn't he come to see you?"

"He comes in and out. Sometimes I know."

"Joel—"

He held up his uninjured hand. "Don't tell me," he said.

Deborah told this to the family that evening at dinner. It was a cool evening and a fire purred softly on the hearth. "Joel wants you to come to see him especially tomorrow," she said to Jared.

"Tomorrow . . ."

"Yes. Tomorrow we discover if he has one good cornea or two."

"He knows . . ."

"I think he does. But you are to go to see him."

"I do. Every day."

"Yes, but this seems to be special."

The next day Jared did go to see him, dressed in street clothes, and the nurse did not recognize the tall, blond man.

"Dr. O'Brien can't have company," she told him. "Only his mother—"

Jared laughed. "I'm his brother," he said. "I am Dr. Jared O'Brien."

She stared at him, going white, then red.

Jared smiled at her, and picked up the chart.

"Are we alone?" asked Joel from the bed.

Jared nodded to the nurse, who went out into the hall. Jared sat down and held Joel's hand. "This may be a tough time, Buddy," he said.

"My eye? I'll handle that. But I wanted to talk to you before we did that. Remember, I told you that I may marry Deb."

Jared laughed. "You'd better," he said.

"But—I thought if you and she—" Joel stammered.

"That could have happened. But not since she's seen you. Especially the way you look now."

"Yeah-yeah. And what about Lutie?"

"She tells me that we will marry. But it still seems the wrong thing to do."

"Are you still thinking of that damned scar?"

Jared's hand went to his cheek. "You'll have one or two of your own," he said gruffly.

"They won't bother Deborah. Or me."

"And the Taussig money—"

"I know you'll use it to send guys in training to the basketball games. We can join with City and become a first-class trauma center."

"You've been thinking."

"What else have I had to do? How long has it been? A week?"

"Something like that."

"As for scars, I decided that we'd have things on a fair and even basis."

"Yes, indeed we will," said Jared, dropping Joel's hand, and standing up.

"Where are you going?" asked Joel in alarm.

"To tell Lutie—"

"After all these years? You'll have to get down on your knees, Buddy."

"I can. I will."

"That I'll want to see."

Jared opened the door. The nurse came in with the cart, Dr. Deb, and a green gown to tie around Jared's neck. He shed his suit jacket.

"You'll see it, Buddy," he told the patient. "Won't he, Dr. Eckman?"

"One eye or two?" asked Joel.

"Whatever it takes," said Deborah and Jared in unison.

195